ROTTEN BODIES
A ZOMBIE SHORT STORY COLLECTION

STEVEN JENKINS

Published in Great Britain in 2015 by
Different Cloud Publishing.
www.steven-jenkins.com

CONTENTS

"For Mum."

FREE BOOK

"If you love scary campfire stories of ghosts, demonology, and all things that go bump in the night, then you'll love this horror collection by author Steven Jenkins."

COLIN DAVIES
Director of BAFTA winning BBC's The Coalhouse.

For a limited time only, you can download a **FREE** copy of Spine - the latest horror collection from Steven Jenkins.

FIND OUT MORE HERE
www.steven-jenkins.com

About the Book

We all fear death's dark spectre, but in a zombie apocalypse, dying is a privilege reserved for the lucky few. There are worse things than a bullet to the brain—*much* worse.

The dead are walking, and they're hungry. Steven Jenkins, bestselling author of *Fourteen Days* and *Burn The Dead*, shares six zombie tales that are rotten for all the right reasons.

Meet Dave, a husband and father with a dirty secret, who quickly discovers that lies aren't only dangerous…they're deadly. Athlete Sarah once ran for glory, but when she finds herself alone on a country road with an injured knee, second place is as good as last. Working in a cremation facility, Rob likes to peek secretly at the faces of his inventory before they're turned to ash. When it comes to workplace health and sanity, however, some rules are better left unbroken. Howard, shovelling coal in the darkness of a Welsh coalmine, knows something's amiss when his colleagues begin to disappear. But it's when the lights come on that things get truly scary.

Six different takes on the undead, from the grotesque to the downright terrifying. But reader beware: as the groans get louder and the twitching starts, you'll be *dying* to reach the final page.

I Am Dead

(First published in Dark Moon Digest)

I don't know who or what killed me—all I know is that I can smell my rotting flesh.

Every joint and muscle aches, and my head is pounding like a bad hangover. Even my fingers hurt and creak when I make a fist. And when I attempt to bend my legs I can feel the fluid burn and swirl around my kneecaps.

I don't remember who I was when I was last breathing, but I do remember the world. I remember the grass, the sky, the buildings, and the...*people*. I could never forget them. I don't remember my previous friends and family; their memory is long gone. No, I only remember the *flesh*. There's something about it that sparks off a hunger inside me that can't be quenched; something that will never cease no matter how much skin and muscle I manage to tear off with my decaying teeth.

But I must eat. Every sense in my dead body is *screaming at me* to satisfy the urge. The urge to feed is primeval; something built into every living creature. A baby needs no lessons on the subject. It knows what it wants, what it needs to survive, even inside the womb. And a starving body will feed on itself to stay alive. It will feast on its own fat, muscle, and eventually its own organs before it's ready to die.

Is that what I have become? Am I a being so ravaged with decay that all there is left for me to do is feed on the flesh of others? Have I no edible tissue of my own? Have I nothing but dead, putrid worm-food to offer?

But what do I care? I feel nothing inside me apart from a relentless hunger. I don't feel an ounce of guilt or pity for anyone I will rip apart and eat. I can't even feel whatever it is that runs through my living corpse. A virus. A voodoo spell. An act of God. Or perhaps the Devil himself. It makes no difference to me. I have no emotion. Even the pain that plagues my body doesn't bother me. Perhaps the agony is just a memory left over from my previous life, not unlike the phantom pain someone feels in a leg that has been amputated.

Despite everything, all my senses seem to be in relatively good working order. My vision still works, although somewhat blurred and distorted. I can still hear my joints make clicking and cracking sounds when I move. But the strangest thing of all, my sense of smell has increased tenfold. I can smell the flesh of the living all around me; the scent of blood pumping around their bodies, filling up every mouth-watering muscle. As for my sense of taste, that has yet to be tested.

I'm looking forward to that the most.

Can I still speak? I'm not sure. I think whatever groan manages to leave my mouth is anything but comprehensive dialogue. It certainly isn't anything that could be understood. Perhaps, like the instinct to feed, I have reverted back to a newborn baby, picking up words as I go. But for all I know, my vocal chords are so withered with decomposition that nothing of sense will ever come out again, no matter how much I learn, or eventually remember.

* * *

Don't know how long I've been this way—days, weeks, months. But with every second that passes this desire to feed on warm flesh is starting to take its toll. It's all I can think about—that and trying to remember which part of the body carries the juiciest meat. The thighs? No, the buttocks. Definitely the buttocks. Not that it matters all that much. I'm fairly sure I could eat a horse in one sitting.

But I'd prefer a human. Don't care what gender. Preferably someone morbidly obese. I could feed on them for days. And the chances of one outrunning me are pretty remote—even with my emaciated legs.

* * *

The time is nearing. I must feed.

I can feel the craving wash over me, tingling through my crumbling body.

I can hear it; smell it.

I can taste it.

If only I could get out of this *fucking coffin*...

Room 503

Chapter 1

I pull up onto the drive, the car rumbling to a halt next to Clare's Mini Cooper. Just before I climb out, before I face the madness of the house, I let out a long groan, both hands still on the steering wheel, clutching tightly.

After a few minutes, I turn to the passenger seat and then pick up the bunch of flowers, unsure if she'll even like them. It's not as if the supermarket has a great selection anyway. But they're pink. She likes pink. That's the main thing.

That's the one thing that I *can* remember.

I give my face a quick check in the mirror, but I hardly recognise the person looking back at me. I see the same disappearing hairline, the same crow's feet and slightly twisted nose. But that's it. The rest is all-new to me. A stranger.

And I *despise him*.

I get out of the car, slam the door, and head towards the house.

As soon as I enter the hallway, the dog greets me, barking, jumping up and down excitedly. "Hello, Chloe," I say in a childlike voice, ruffling the top of her fluffy white coat. "Where is everyone, girl?"

"Daddy!" I hear Katie yell. Suddenly I see her bolt out of the kitchen towards me, her blonde hair bobbing up and down like waves.

I kneel down and catch her in a hug. "Hello, my beautiful little girl. How was school today?"

"It was good. We learned about Autumn. And Mrs Hinsley took us on a nature hunt."

"Really?" I pick her up off the floor and carry her back towards the kitchen. "What did you find?"

"We found some brown leaves, some sycamore seeds. *Oh*, and we saw a squirrel."

"That's awesome, sweetheart," I say, kissing her on the forehead. "I'm proud of you."

Inside the kitchen, I see Clare standing by the table, holding a large white pot, oven gloves covering her hands. She has already laid out three placemats and bowls.

"That smells nice," I tell her, as I lower Katie onto a chair. "What's for dinner?"

She sets the pot onto the centre of the table and removes the oven gloves. "Beef casserole."

"Sounds great," I say, walking over to her and kissing her on the lips. "These are for you." I hand over the flowers.

Clare smiles as she takes them from me. "For me? You shouldn't have. What's the occasion?"

I shrug. "No occasion. Just wanted to do something nice. No big deal. Are they all right?"

"Of course they are." She kisses me again. "I love them, Dave. They're beautiful." She takes the flowers over to the sink, fills the drainer with water, and puts them in. "I'll put them in a vase after dinner."

Sitting next to Katie, I notice the newspaper at the side of the table. I grab it and start to read the front page. "*Jesus*, this infection's not going away."

"What's that, Dave?" Clare asks from behind me.

"This infection thing. They say it's over here now."

"I know. It's been all over the TV. They've had to close some schools in England and Scotland."

"Really? That bad, is it?"

"*Yeah*," Clare replies, sitting at the table. "The guy on the news said that some schools over here might be closing too."

"*Bloody hell*. Sounds like a lot of panic over nothing."

"I don't know, Dave, if they're thinking about closing the schools—"

"Yeah, but that's all just paranoia, health and safety gone mad. Remember when it was swine flu? Remember how crazy everything got? They talked about closing them then. And that blew over."

"I hope so. I'd hate for Katie to have to miss out on something."

"Clare, she's five. I hardly think she's gonna miss out on anything vital."

"Yeah, I know, but if it does close, then who's going to look after her? Have you thought of that?"

"We'll cross that bridge if and when we come to it. Right now, all that matters is eating that delicious casserole." I turn to Katie. "Isn't that right, sweetheart?"

Katie nods her little head enthusiastically.

Smiling, Clare scoops out the piping-hot food with a ladle, and then starts to fill each bowl.

* * *

"What story would you like?" I ask Katie as she lies, tucked up in her bed, *Tinkerbell* quilt pulled to her chest. "How about the one with the dinosaur."

She shakes her head quickly.

"No? All right. What about the *Gruffalo*? You like that one."

"I don't like that anymore."

I sit on the edge of the bed. "Why? What's wrong with it?"

"It's too scary."

"No, it's not, sweetheart. It's funny."

"No, it's about a monster. I don't like monsters."

"You mustn't be afraid of monsters. They're not real."

"Yes they are."

"*No*. They're just from stories. They're made up. The only scary things we have are crocodiles and sharks. And they live far, far away—on the other side of the world."

Katie nods, but I can tell by her eyes that she's still unconvinced. "Okay, little lady, how about I check your bedroom for monsters? Would that help?"

"Okay, Daddy. But you have to check under the bed first. That's where they like to hide."

"Under the bed, is it? All right." I get up, go down on one knee, and then inspect underneath. "No monsters under here."

"Check the wardrobe."

"All right, you're the boss." I walk over to the wardrobe and open the doors. "All I see are clothes and shoes. Absolutely zero monsters." I shut the doors and turn to her. "Happy now?"

Katie shakes her head. "Don't forget behind the curtains. I'm sure I saw some monster feet there."

"Monster feet? And what did they look like?"

"Purple with long yellow toenails."

"Purple with long yellow toenails? Are you sure they're not Mummy's?"

Katie giggles. "No. Mummy has pretty feet."

"Are you positive? I saw Mummy's toenails earlier, and I'm *sure* they were long and yellow."

Katie laughs again. It makes me smile as I pull open the curtains. "Got you! *Oh*, there's no one here." I walk back over to the bed. "Happy now, sweetheart?"

Nodding, she hugs her soft elephant toy. "Can Chloe sleep in my room tonight? Keep me company? She'll bark if there's monsters."

"No. Sorry, sweetheart. You know she's not allowed upstairs. She smells too much."

"I don't mind the smell."

"Yeah, but your mother and I do. So no dogs allowed. Now which bedtime story would you like? Maybe something *without* any monsters."

Sitting up in bed, she points to a book that's resting on her toy box. "That one. The Three Billy-Goats Gruff."

I pick it up and take it over to her. "But this one has a troll in it."

"Yes, but the big goat throws him in the river."

I shake my head with a look of disappointment on my face. "Thanks a bunch. Now you've ruined the ending for me."

Katie chuckles again.

* * *

Walking down the stairs, I notice that Clare has put the flowers into a vase and set it down on the hallway shelf, next to the photo of us in Disneyland Paris. For a bunch of cheap, supermarket flowers, they don't look half-bad. Not that I'm an expert on gardening, but it's not like these are the first flowers that I've bought for Clare. And they definitely won't be the last. The only problem is I'm pretty sure she's figured out by now that she only gets them when I'm awash with guilt. I can see the suspicion in her eyes every time I hand a bunch over, or she comes home from work carrying ones I've had delivered.

I should just stop sending them, if it's that obvious. But I can't help myself. The guilt starts to creep over me like a rash, and I find myself at the flower stand, reaching into my jacket for my wallet.

I enter the living room and sit next to Clare. She's watching some cookery show, and Chloe is sleeping by her feet.

"Did she go down all right?" she asks, turning to me.

"Fine. Just read her a story, and she was out like a light."

Clare smiles. "Good."

"So how was your day?"

Clare picks up the remote and mutes the TV. "Not too bad. Pretty quiet this time of year. Once summer's out of the way, people stop buying houses. God knows why. A house is a house. Shouldn't matter what time of year it is."

"Yeah. Exactly. So what's happening with that receptionist? Did your boss get 'round to firing her?"

"*Yep*. She left last Wednesday. Packed up and was escorted out of the building."

"So it was her stealing the money?"

"Yeah. She admitted it. Once Peter threatened to call the police, she soon changed her tune."

"Bloody hell. That must have been an awkward day at the office."

Clare nods, her eyebrows raised. "Tell me about it." She then puts both her feet up and rests them on my thighs, disturbing Chloe in the process. "So how was your day? Anything interesting happen?"

I snort. "What, in my job? That'll be the day."

Clare grins. "You must have something juicy to tell me. We haven't had a chance to chat for almost a week."

I shake my head. "Clare, you married an accountant. Nothing interesting ever happens to accountants. Unless you think sending out Tax Return reminders to your clients is interesting. I certainly don't."

"Then why don't you do something interesting with your life."

"I didn't say I didn't enjoy my job; it's just always uneventful. At least with your job you have a lot of staff floating around, all with something to say. All I have is Neil to talk to. And he's a borderline alcoholic."

Clare's eyes light up. "*There*—some real gossip."

"Well, I suppose. But you already knew that."

"Did I?"

"Yeah. You did," I reply, trying to conceal my annoyance. She never listens to a word I say—more concerned with watching some dickhead on TV, baking a bloody pie.

"Oh, well, I can't remember. Maybe you did."

Maybe?

"Well, *anyway*," Clare continues, clearly sensing another argument brewing on the horizon, "shall we watch TV? The grand finale of *Masterchef* is on."

I sigh quietly, but loud enough for her to hear.

"Okay, so we'll watch something *you* want to watch then."

"No, it's fine. You can watch whatever you want," I say, glancing over at the clock on the

17

mantelpiece. "I need an early night anyway. Got a seven o' clock start in the morning, and then I'm off to that training course straight after."

"Training course? Since when?"

"Since four months ago."

"I don't remember any training course."

"I told you when I booked the bloody thing," I snap. "Don't you retain *any information* at all, Clare?"

"Don't be an ass, Dave. I've got a lot on my plate. You can't expect me to remember every little thing you tell me."

I don't reply; just try to calm the beast that's looming in the pit of my stomach.

Apart from the rain outside, lightly hitting the window, the living room falls silent. I can tell that neither one of us wants another fight. I know *I* don't. There's nothing worse than going to bed like this, with a thick, murky atmosphere. I hate it.

But why the hell is it always me who has to clear the air, has to apologise? Why can't she, for once in her life, just step up—even if she thinks that she's in the right? *I* bloody do. I know *I* can suck it up and tell her how sorry I am, even if I know *damn well* that it's her fault.

So bloody stubborn.

Chloe walks over to my feet, her head resting on my right knee. I stroke her soft coat and watch as her eyes close with pleasure. The life of a dog— so much simpler.

"Look," I say, breaking the silence, "I'll be gone for the night. It's in Crawley so it'll take me a good three hours to drive up."

"What about taking Katie swimming in the morning? You promised her. She's been so excited."

I sigh, pissed off that it had completely slipped my mind. "Well, I'll be back by Saturday afternoon. It's only for one night. And if I'm running late then I'll take her Sunday instead."

"She's got a birthday party on Sunday."

"Then I'll make sure that I leave first thing Saturday morning."

"*Fine*," Clare replies, sharply, lifting her legs off my lap and putting them back on the carpet. She picks up the TV remote and puts the sound back on, not even looking at me.

I shake my head in frustration. "I'm going up for a shower and then to bed."

She doesn't respond.

"I'll see you when I get back then," I say, exiting the living room and shaking my head in annoyance.

CHAPTER 2

I wake moments before my alarm goes off. It's five in the morning, and I'm not really sure if I slept a wink at all. I remember drifting off around three, but it couldn't have been more than a few minutes' doze.

There's a faint glow from the moonlight seeping through the curtains. Quietly I climb out of bed, trying to make as little noise and movement with the mattress as possible. Once I'm standing, I see that Clare is fast asleep. Either that, or she's faking. Wouldn't be the first time. She can be quite the actor.

Grabbing my overnight bag from the front of the wardrobe, I tiptoe towards the bedroom door. I stop at Clare's side of the bed and stare at her subtle dimples on permanently rosy cheeks, her brown hair still tucked behind her right ear, the soft olive skin on her arm as it drapes over her chest. It pains me to leave like this, with unresolved issues. But what's to resolve? It was only a little tiff. It's not like we haven't bickered before. Leaning over her, with the intention to kiss her on the cheek, I stop, and then retract my head. Can't risk waking her. It's too early. And what if she's still mad with me?

I'll see her tomorrow.

I head quietly along the landing into Katie's room. It's dimly lit with her nightlight on the bedside cabinet. Her tiny body is wrapped up tightly with the quilt, her hands still grasping her elephant toy like it was a real animal. Smiling, I kneel beside her and gently stroke her hair, and then kiss her on the cheek. I whisper that I love her and then head for the door.

"Daddy," I hear a whisper as I step out onto the landing. Turning back, I see Katie's eye wide open.

Returning to her bedside, I crouch down by her head. "Hello," I whisper. "Did I wake you, sweetheart?"

Katie nods her head. "Is it morning yet?"

"No, not quite. It's still early. Try to get a little more sleep. You've got school today."

"Where are you going, Daddy?"

"I've got to go into work for a few hours and then Daddy's got to go to Crawley."

"What's Crawley?"

"It's a place near London."

"Is it far away?"

"Yes. It's quite far. We're in Birmingham so if I drive it'll take me about three hours. Maybe even longer. That's why I have to stay there tonight. Daddy's got to do a course. But Daddy doesn't want to go. I'd much rather go to school with you."

"Are you still taking me swimming on Saturday?"

"Of course I am. I wouldn't miss it for the world. That's why I'll be leaving first thing Saturday morning so I can be back to take you in the afternoon. Is that okay? Can you wait that long?"

Katie nods.

"Good girl," I whisper, stroking her soft hair. "Well, Daddy's got to go to work now so try to get some sleep. And I'll see you tomorrow."

"Okay, Daddy."

I tuck the quilt around Katie's body and then kiss her on the forehead. "Love you, sweetheart."

"Love you, too."

Even after five years, my heart still melts when I hear those words. I'm not even sure if she understands the power they hold.

But who cares.

I blow her a kiss and then leave the room.

As I pass our bedroom door, I contemplate going in, giving Clare a kiss goodbye. But I don't. It'll only make today all the more difficult.

* * *

I managed to get out of the office by eleven, missing the morning rush by a good couple of hours. Pointless heading off any earlier; the motorway is always manic around eight or nine o' clock. The roads have been pretty clear, apart from a crash by the Oxford turn-off. I thought about stopping for a coffee or a bite to eat at lunchtime, but I was making great time.

It's now going on two and I'm about three miles from Crawley. I did consider using the Satnav, but this isn't the first time I've been here, so I should know these streets by now. Although, every time I'm up here, I get lost and stumble across the hotel by sheer luck.

Just as I think I'm making great time, I'm hit with another traffic jam. Can't see what the delay is. Just see a lot of police and paramedics about a half a mile up. Probably a crash. There doesn't seem to be any movement at all, and I've seen at least two cars do a three-point turn to get out of the queue. I decide to do the same. I reverse the car a little and then swing it 'round and head in the other direction, tyres squealing.

Once I'm a distance away from the traffic, I pull over and enter the hotel's postcode into the Satnav. There's bound to be another way into town.

CHAPTER 3

After two more traffic jams and three wrong turns, I finally get to The Winchester Hotel at the centre of Crawley. I park my car at the back of the hotel and make my way inside the building.

The lobby looks pretty upmarket; revolving door, gigantic windows, shiny cream floor-tiles, large marble reception desk, open-plan bar and kitchen to the left, internet room and lifts to the right—stunning foreign woman standing behind the desk.

"Hello, Sir," the dark-haired woman says, with a strong, Eastern European accent, smiling with perfect white teeth, skin light brown. "Welcome to The Winchester. How can I help you?"

I drop my bag on the floor and lean against the desk. "Oh, hi, I have a reservation under Michael John."

The woman looks up the name on her computer. After a few seconds, she nods her head. "Yes. I have a Mr and Mrs John, staying for one night, double deluxe suite, breakfast included. Paid in full. Are those details correct, Sir?"

"Yes, that's right. Mrs John will be joining me shortly."

"That's fine, Mr John. I just need a credit card for any additional bar and room charges."

"No problem," I reply, handing her my credit card.

She swipes it on the machine, and then gives me a white key-card. "Your room is ready. It's on the fifth floor. Room 503." She points to the right. "The elevator is just over there. Our breakfast buffet is available between 6:00 A.M. and 10:00 A.M., served on the third floor."

"Thank you."

"Is there anything else I can do for you?"

I smile, shaking my head. "No, that's great. Can you send Mrs John up when she arrives? She shouldn't be long."

"No problem, Sir. Enjoy your stay."

Picking up my bag, I start to make my way over to the lifts. "Don't worry...I will."

* * *

I throw the bag on the floor, collapse onto the king-size bed, pick up the remote control, and then point it at the massive TV screen, mounted on the wall directly in front of me. The news is the first that comes on. I'm not really paying much attention. Something about that infection again. Same old shit. I switch over the channel, and it's the same report. "Bloody hell," I mumble. "Change the record." Just as I'm about to switch to another station, I hear a knock at the door. I mute the TV and leap from the bed like an excited child. I get to the door, check my hair and teeth in the mirror, and then open it.

"Hello, *Mr John*," Jenni says in a playful voice, light blue suitcase by her feet, red skirt, black jacket, and a big smile on her face.

"Hello, *Mrs John*. So glad you could join me."

Jenni laughs and then kisses me as I drag her inside by her hand.

I close the door and take the suitcase from her. "What the hell's *in* this?" I ask her, frowning. "We're only here one bloody night."

She walks around the room, clearly inspecting the quality. "A girl's gotta look her best, doesn't she?" She pokes her head into the bathroom, and then nods. "Not bad, Dave. Not bad at all. This'll do nicely. Better than that last shithole you brought us to."

"A shithole? It wasn't that bad."

"Dave, it didn't even have room service. *Or* a shower."

I sit on the bed. "Well, this place *does* have room service. And we're gonna need it, too—'cause we ain't leaving this room all night."

"What? Not even for a drink in the lobby bar?"

I shake my head. "What's the point? We've got everything we need right here. Room service, a shower," I slap the mattress with the palm of my hand. "A king-size bed."

Jenni shrugs her shoulders, scans the room with her big blue eyes, and brushes her blonde hair from her face. "Sounds like you've got it all figured out then."

Reaching forward, I take hold of her hands and pull her slender body towards me. "Why don't I just tear off that red shirt," I pull her even closer, both hands now clutching her firm ass, squeezing hard, "and fuck you right here, right this minute?"

Jenni doesn't retort. Instead she shoves me backwards so that I'm lying on the bed, with my feet still on the floor. She then follows me down, her hips pressed against mine. She kisses me on the lips, her fingers running through my hair.

"I've missed you," I whisper as I glide my hands up her skirt, and start to peel down her panties.

"I've missed you, too."

CHAPTER 4

I'm lying on the bed, under the quilt covers, Jenni's arm draped over my bare chest, staring at the muted TV. It's still showing that same news report. I can't change the channel; the remote control is lost somewhere, buried under the mounds of clothes, scattered across the carpet and bed.

"So how's work?" Jenni asks, her eyes still closed.

"I thought you'd fallen asleep."

She shakes her head. "No. Just resting my eyes. Women don't fall asleep after sex. That's men."

"Well, *I'm* still awake."

She opens her eyes and sits up, her bare back against the leather headboard. "I know. I'm as shocked as you are." She then picks up her half-empty champagne flute from the bedside table, and takes a slow sip. "So how's little Katie doing?"

"She's great," I reply, struggling to hide the suspicion in my voice.

"That's good." She takes another swig of her drink. "And Clare? How's she doing?"

I sit up in bed, throwing her a scowl. "Do we really have to talk about my family?"

"Why?" Jenni asks, a mischievous smirk on her face. "Feeling guilty or something?"

"*Well*, 'course I feel guilty. Who wouldn't? But I'd rather not be thinking about them right now."

"No need to get touchy, Dave. I was only teasing."

"I know that, Jen, but I'd rather be focused on you right now." I place my hand over hers. "Not my family."

"Fine then—*Grumpy*," she replies with a smile. "It's a good job that frown makes you look handsome."

I relax my brow. "What frown? I'm happy. Why wouldn't I be? I'm in this stunning hotel room, with an even more stunning woman. What's there to frown about?"

She leans over and kisses my lips. "You're lucky I'm a sucker for compliments."

Beaming, I grab the champagne bottle from the bedside cabinet, and top up her glass. "How's *that* for service?"

"Not bad. I could get used to this."

"I'm just trying to get you drunk, that's all."

"Well it's working," she replies, taking a huge swig. "Can't get too drunk though, got an afternoon shift tomorrow."

"Oh, right. How is life at the clothes shop these days? Stimulating I bet."

"It's all right I suppose. Don't really like to moan too much."

I throw her a look to suggest the opposite. "Really? You?"

"Well, maybe before, but I've matured since the last time I saw you."

"In two months? Bloody hell, that was quick."

She nudges me teasingly. "Cheeky bastard. *I have.* I was getting sick of hearing all the other staff going on about how hard and underappreciated we all are. So now I've tuned it out and stopped bitching. It's only a clothes shop, after all. It's not rocket science."

"Well that *is* mature, Jen. It's about time, too. You'll be the ripe old age of thirty in three years."

She nudges me again. "Piss off. Don't remind me." She finishes her glass and climbs out of bed.

"Where you off to?"

"Just going out on the balcony for a cigarette," she replies, slipping a white bathrobe over her naked body. "You want one?"

"No, thanks. Those things'll kill you."

"You only live once, Dave," she says, drawing the thin white curtains. She then slides open the glass door and disappears out into the night.

I grab my champagne glass from the bedside cabinet and swallow its contents in one gulp.

"Hey, Dave?" I hear Jenni say from outside.

"Yeah?"

"There's something going on out here."

"What do you mean?"

"It looks like a riot. There's a load of police all over the street."

"Really?" I say, not even trying to conceal my excitement to witness a little action. Front-row seats too. Climbing out of bed, I grab my bathrobe and join Jenni out on the small balcony. Down on the street, I see two police vans and a row of at least fifteen police, armed with batons, shields and full riot-gear. Directly opposite, just fifty or so metres away, I see at least sixty or seventy, men and women, staggering towards the wall of officers.

We're a little too high up to know for sure, but from here they don't look like your average football hooligans, especially the women.

"What the hell is going on down there?" Jenni asks, leaning over the railing.

"I don't know. Looks pretty serious though. Haven't heard about any rioting on the news."

"Is there a football match on or something?"

I shrug my shoulders. "Maybe. But none of them have football jerseys on."

"Yeah. You're right. And why are they moving like that? Are they all drunk?"

"Don't know. Must be. But why bring the riot police? They don't even look that aggressive. They're just walking."

"STAY BACK!" I hear a police officer scream through a megaphone. The loud voice does nothing to deter the crowd. He shouts again, this time with even more punch. Still no effect.

What the hell is wrong with them?

Suddenly the rioters start to bolt towards the police, howling like wild animals.

"Jesus Christ!" I blurt out, taking hold of Jenni's arm. "Did you see that?"

"I know. What the hell are they doing? Do you think we're safe up—?"

The sound of gunfire fills the street, echoing off the walls of the adjacent buildings. I drop down to the balcony floor, yanking Jenni down with me. Pulling her close, I try to cover both our heads with my arms.

"Fucking hell!" Jenni cries; her words muffled by my bathrobe sleeve. "Was that a gun?"

"I think it was," I reply, my voice lined with panic. I crawl forward a little so I can see over the edge of the balcony.

"Where are you going?" she asks, clearly petrified.

"I just need to see what's happening."

"Don't be stupid. Get back inside the room."

She's right; I know she is. But I can't fight that curious demon, surging through my body. But when I hear another barrage of gunfire, and a deafening human shriek, we both scurry on our hands and knees, back through the glass sliding doors, to the safety of room 503.

What the hell is going on down there?" Jenni says, getting to her feet, racing to the bed, away from the window.

"I don't know, Jen," I reply, my back against the wall beside the window. "Sounds pretty bad out there."

I watch Jenni as she sits on the edge of the bed, eyes wide with fear, and all I can think about is returning to the balcony, re-joining the action. I can't help it. Don't know if it's a male thing or just sheer stupidity, but I can't help myself from gawking.

And so, stupid or not, I drop down to my hands and knees and start to crawl back out onto the balcony.

"Dave!" Jenni shouts. "What the hell are you doing? Get back in here!"

I shush her as my hands touch the tiled surface of the balcony. At the railing, staying low, I can see down onto the street. There are now even more people, some running, others ambling, across the pavement and road, maybe a hundred, coming in all directions. From this angle, I can just about see that the police vans are still there. I'm too low to see where the riot police are. Need to see more. Grabbing the railing, I gingerly pull myself up about half way.

"Oh shit," I mumble when I see some of the riot police, pinned to the floor by groups of people. What the hell are they doing? I can't see any fists being thrown.

Jesus Christ, is that one biting down on that cop's leg?

I stand up.

Fuck me, he is!

Without even realising, I'm now leaning right over the edge of the railing, looking down at the horror, unable to believe my own eyes. Police officers are being torn to shreds by madmen and women—right in front of the hotel!

This can't be happening!

"Dave!" I hear Jenni yell. At first I ignore her, struggling to take in the chaos down below, but then she calls my name again, this time even louder.

I snap out of my shocked, frozen state, and leave the balcony.

"You need to see this," she says, standing in front of the TV screen, clutching the remote control.

There's a news reporter on the screen, standing outside a school somewhere in London. *"Police Chiefs are urging everyone to stay in a safe, secure place,"* the reporter says, *"with all doors and windows locked. If you're travelling on the road, then you must, at all costs, stay away from any built-up areas such as cities and large towns. Schools, like this one behind me, have been evacuated, the staff and pupils taken to secure locations. The local police in each area are working to keep the infected isolated and behind the barricades..."*

"What the hell does he mean, 'infected'?"

I shush her abruptly, trying to listen to the rest of the report.

"At this moment in time there is no vaccine, so Disease Control is recommending that if you or a family member have been bitten by anyone assumed to be infected, you need to be quarantined immediately..."

Stomach churning, I have to sit down on the edge of the bed as the reporter continues to talk about quarantines and infections, and all things that aren't meant to happen in the UK.

Katie.

"I need to leave this hotel right now," I say, firmly, getting up off the bed and gathering up my jeans from the floor.

"You can't leave," she demands, pointing to the TV. "The news said that we need to stay inside."

I slip my jeans on, nearly falling in the process. "I can't just stay here and wait, Jen. She might be in danger." I find my shirt draped over the dressing-table chair. "They both might be."

"And what about me? You can't just leave me here on my own."

"Then come with me," I suggest, buttoning up my shirt.

"With that going on outside? Don't be stupid. It's too dangerous."

"Look, Jen, I'm leaving. I've got no choice. What if something's happened to them?"

Jenni picks up my mobile phone from the bedside cabinet and throws it to me. "Call her then."

I look at her suspiciously for a moment, but then find Clare's number and hit the call button. Holding it up to my ear, I wait anxiously for the call to connect, unable to make eye contact with Jenni. After a few seconds, I hear a recorded message telling me that the *'network is busy. Please try again later'*. Immediately I try again. Then again, until finally giving in and launching the phone on the bed. "Shit!"

"Try your house phone."

"We don't have a house phone anymore."

"What about your dad? Maybe he can check on them."

"My dad is seventy-eight and lives in a nursing home," I say, almost annoyed that she didn't already know that.

I sit on the chair and slip my shoes on.

"Look, Dave, please don't go. At least wait a while. Maybe those people outside will move on."

I ponder for a moment, trying to rationalise everything. But I can't. How can I? I've just seen a load of *maniacs* tear pieces out of a cop. There's nothing to rationalise.

Just as I'm about to race out the door, to hell with Jenni's advice, I notice the room phone on the bedside cabinet. I race over to it and pick up the receiver. I push the number for reception, but I'm met with an engaged-tone. "Shit!" I slam the receiver down in anger. I sit on the bed, hot and bothered, sweat beads collecting on my brow. I take a deep breath to calm the frantic, hysterical beast raging in my gut.

After a few seconds, I try the phone again.

The same.

My grip around the receiver tightening, I try one more time.

This time the call goes through.

"*Yes?*" a man says.

No '*Welcome to The Winchester Hotel.*' No '*How can I be of service?*'

That can't be a good sign.

CHAPTER 5

"Sir, I'm afraid that it's not safe to leave the hotel at this moment," the receptionist says through the speakerphone. "We are asking that all guests remain inside their rooms with the doors locked."

"What the hell's going on down there?" I ask. "I saw a bunch of police officers get taken down by a load of psychos a few minutes ago, just outside the hotel entrance."

"I know, Sir. We're well aware of the problem. But I assure you that everything is under control. We have the place locked down. Nothing's coming in or out until help arrives."

"And how long will that be?"

"We're told that police backup is on its way. They should be with us within minutes. But for the time being, as I've already said, you need to stay in your room. And just to warn you, we will be shutting down the lights in the entire hotel."

"What for?"

"We've been instructed by the police to shut down anything that might attract attention from the infected."

"What about the back doors? Can I at least—"

"Sir, I'm going to need to keep all phone lines free until the police arrive. We'll call up if there are any further developments."

The phone goes dead.

"Shit!"

I put the receiver back in its position and groan loudly. What the hell am I meant to do now? I feel so helpless. I hate feeling like this. In the dark. So powerless. It's just not me.

I glance at Jenni; she's leaning against the chair, still wearing her bathrobe, her eyes gleaming with worry.

"So what now?" she asks.

I shake my head. "I don't know, Jen. I can't go out there with all that shit going on. But I can't just sit here and do nothing while Clare and Katie could be in danger."

"Don't be an idiot!" she snaps. "You're no good to anyone dead."

"I'm not an idiot. I have to risk it. Katie's only five. She needs me."

"Yeah, but your precious Clare is with her," she says, a hint of venom in her tone.

"Jesus, Jen, without getting through to her I have no way of knowing if she even *has her*."

Jenni starts to pick up her clothes from the floor and bed. "Do what you want, Dave. You always do."

"What the hell's wrong with you? I'd never let any harm come to you. I love you, Jen."

"I know that's bullshit," she blurts out, slipping her skirt on.

"No, it's not. I've always loved you."

"Like Clare?"

Getting up off the bed, I go to her, take her hand. She pulls out of my grip. "It's different with Clare," I say. "She's Katie's mother. I don't want

38

my daughter to go through what I went through when my parents split." I take her hand again, but this time she doesn't resist. "Okay?"

She doesn't answer, struggling to meet my eyes.

"Look, how about we both make a run for the car?"

"With those people outside? Are you nuts?"

"My car's parked at the back of the hotel. We can use one of the fire exits."

Jenni shakes her head. "No. I'm not leaving this room. And nor should you. At least until someone comes to rescue us. You heard what the news said."

"Look, I'm not staying—"

Suddenly the lights go out. And the TV shuts off.

Jenni moves in close to me. "Oh shit!"

"Don't worry. He said they might go out."

"I don't like this, Dave. I'm scared out of my mind."

"Stay here for a minute."

"Where are you going?" she asks, her words broken by fear. "Don't leave me!"

"I'm not going anywhere. I'm just going out onto the balcony."

"Why?"

"I just need to see if those people have gone. Maybe switching off the lights has started to work."

"Okay. But be careful, Dave."

"Don't worry. Just stay put."

I kiss her on the cheek and then step out onto the balcony. It's started to rain a little. Let's hope it pisses down. Maybe the bad weather will dissuade them. Peering over the railing, I see a horde of people gathered at the front of the hotel, howling like starving dogs, fists pounding at the entrance door and windows. The remains of several dead police officers are scattered along the road and pavement, and there are more infected staggering towards the crowd like wounded drunks. What the hell do they want? Was the receptionist right? Were they just attracted to the lights of the hotel? Maybe they'll leave now, disperse, find somewhere else to terrorise.

Anywhere but here.

Katie. Clare

Please God let them be safe. Please say that she got out of school safely. Images of infected people, beating down my front door, storming Katie's bedroom while she sleeps fill my head. Shuddering at the very notion, I can feel the frustration, the anger bubble up inside. I need to get back to them. I'm helpless here. I couldn't live with myself if anything happened to them.

Coming here was a *big* mistake.

CHAPTER 6

I try to call Clare's phone again, but still only get that same message that the network is busy. I feel like tossing the mobile off the balcony in rage. But I won't. If it's really as bad as the news claims, then I'll need my phone now more than ever.

"Things are getting crazy," Jenni says, looking down at her phone.

"Are you on the Internet?"

She nods. "They're saying that these infected people are supposed to be dead."

Frowning in puzzlement, I sit next to her on the edge of the bed, eyes hovering over her mobile screen. "What do you mean? That the virus was meant to kill them but hasn't? Well that's great news then."

"*No.* They're saying that one bite kills you, and then in a few minutes, you wake up as one of those madmen outside."

"What? That's ridiculous."

"Apparently the virus has mutated. They're saying that it can take over the host's body even after death."

"That's stupid, Jen. What bloody website are you on?" I ask, trying to snatch the phone from her. "Give me that thing."

"*Piss off, Dave,*" she replies, moving the phone out of reach. "It's real. I'm on the main news site. It's on all of them."

I let out a chuckle. "For Christ's sake, Jen. Put the Internet off. Don't waste your battery on bullshit like that. Dead people can't just walk around. They're bloody *dead*. It's not *Weekend at Bernie's* for Christ's sake."

"It's not dead people walking around. Once you're dead, *you're dead*. They're saying it's the *virus* that's doing the walking."

"Jesus, Jen, some of those madmen were *sprinting*. They looked pretty lively to me. This is obviously some new rabies strain. Shit like that spreads like wildfire. Now switch off your Internet. We'll need our batteries."

"Why? I've got my phone charger in my bag."

"So how the hell are you meant to plug it in? The hotel's power's been turned off."

"*Shit*. I forgot." She switches off the Internet and sets the phone down on the bedside cabinet. "How long do you think they'll keep the power off?"

"Don't know. At least until those infected people leave. But if they don't, who knows how long those glass entrance doors will hold."

"Don't say that, Dave. I'm already going out of my mind with worry."

I stand up from the bed. "Then let's get the hell out of here, Jen. I feel boxed in. I can't stand it. We'll be better off making a run for the car park. Maybe the back exit is clear."

"No, Dave. It's too risky. We're safer up here. At least that door has a lock on it. And if these people *are dead*, then maybe they won't be able to use the stairs."

I snort. "Really, Jen? Dead? You don't seriously believe that, do you?"

"I don't know what to believe!" she snaps, eyes filled with tears. "All I know is that I'm not leaving this room until the police get here!"

"*Okay. Okay.* Calm down, Jen. No one's gonna make you leave."

"Good!"

"How about this then: we go downstairs and just check if the car park is clear?"

"I said 'no', Dave, why aren't you listening to me?"

"*Okay*, what about if I just go down on my own then?"

"What, and leave me up here alone? No way!"

"No. I didn't mean that. If the coast is clear, then I'll come back up for you. And we can get the hell out of this bloody hotel." I reach into my jeans pocket, pull out my car keys, and throw them on the bed next to her. "I'll even give you my car keys to prove that I'll come straight back."

Jenni picks up the keys and falls silent, clearly mulling over her decision.

"It's the best option. I promise you," I reassure her. "We're caged in up here."

"*Exactly.* Away from those people."

"What if they do end up storming the building? We've got to be smart about this, Jen." I point over to the room door. "They could burst through there. Lock or no lock. *Easily.* Especially if there's enough

43

of them. And then what? We've got nothing to barricade the door with; no planks of wood, no nails. We don't have any weapons, no way to escape, other than off the balcony. And I don't know about you, Jen, but I don't fancy jumping five storeys down onto solid concrete. Do you?"

Jenni goes quiet for a few seconds, and then lets out a drawn out sigh. "Okay. I get your point. But be quick, Dave. *Please*."

"Don't worry. I will. I'll be five minutes. Tops."

I kiss her on the lips and then head for the door.

"Please be careful, Dave."

"I will."

"I love you."

I open the door, "I love you, too," and then step out.

There are a few emergency lights dotted along the ceiling, dimly lighting the corridor. I can't see any people. With the hotel being this dark, this still, I almost feel like the place is deserted and that Jen and me are the only two guests in the whole building. Should I knock on someone's door, see if they've got a better plan than to creep downstairs to see if the coast is clear? Doubtful. I'm guessing that everyone is probably just sitting tight, waiting for this thing to blow over. I'm sure it will. Whatever it is. The government isn't going to let some virus get out of hand. We're not West Africa. We're Great Britain, for Christ's sake!

I follow the lights down towards the lifts. I know they're not working, but the stairs are never too far from them. The darkness of the corridor is creeping me out a little; never been in a hotel with the power out. It's disturbing.

At the lifts, I see a sign for the stairs just above a door. I push it open and see the landing of the fifth floor, with the staircase lit only by a wall-mounted emergency light. Making my way down, the sound of my footsteps on the steel steps echoes around me, causing me to tighten up nervously. Who knows if one of those things is actually inside the hotel? Have to be quiet. Can't risk it. I tiptoe down the remaining flights until I reach the ground floor. There is a small glass panel in the door; I peek through directly into the lobby. A sudden rush of terror hits me when I notice, to the left of me, the entrance doors—with a mass of infected people pressed heavily against the glass. I quickly move away from the door and lean against the wall, heart racing, brow glazed in sweat.

I need to think.

There must be a fire exit. Or a service entrance. I'm sure I saw one when I parked the car. Just have to slip past the receptionist and find a door. Can't be that hard.

I look through the glass panel into the lobby again. Just like the rest of the hotel, it's lit only by a few emergency lights; one, unfortunately, positioned just above the entrance doors, and the other, even worse, on the wall by the reception desk. My view to the desk is mostly hidden, so I push the door open slightly and poke my head out a little. I can just about see a set of feet and legs, clearly sitting on the floor behind the desk. I'm guessing it's the poor receptionist, or a security guard, armed with only a walkie-talkie and a telephone. Unlucky bastard. He definitely pulled the short straw tonight. I creep out of the stairwell and carefully close the door. Keeping low to the lobby floor, I skulk towards a door. Just before the reception desk there's a sign, which reads *Staff Only*, above a glass panel. Silently, I get to the door. I push it open, praying that the hinges don't squeak. This is an upmarket hotel, so they don't. I slip through the door, and I'm in a pitch-black corridor. Just down a few metres there's a green light. All I can hear is the sound of my breathing as I approach it.

Is that an exit door?

On the left side of the steel door there is a small window. I sigh in relief as I press my face against the glass. I can't believe my luck—it leads directly out into the customer car park. Thank God! Scanning the outside area, I can't see anyone; no hotel staff, no police, and no infected people. Completely deserted, just a few puddles as the rain comes down, and about thirty parked cars. I grab the door handle and start to pull. It won't budge. *Locked!* But then I notice a deadbolt at the top. I roll my eyes and slide the bolt across. Pulling on the handle again, it still won't open. "*What the shit*," I mumble quietly in frustration, examining the door again for any other locks. I don't see any so I try again. After a few seconds of straining, there's a faint scraping sound as the door slowly moves from the frame. It's just a little stiff. No big deal. I pull and pull until finally the door flies open—me along with it.

Suddenly a deafening alarm starts to wail.

It's the door! Oh fuck!

Panicked, I start to push the door shut. It feels even stiffer as it rubs against the floor. I'm about twelve or so inches from shutting it when I see something through the window. A figure, sprinting past the cars towards me. Then another. And another.

Jesus Christ, there're a dozen of them!

The force of multiple bodies slamming against the door causes me to let go for a second. The sound of the alarm screeching, mixed with the sound of people screaming like lunatics, sends an unbearable shudder of horror through my body. I push with every ounce of strength I have, and the door creeps nearer to closing. But the sheer weight of their bodies, their fingers, arms, squeezing through the doorway causes the gap to widen. I keep pushing, trying not to look at the faces, but it's impossible. The grey, soulless eyes, skin a light purple, bruised and bloodied, teeth foaming, snarling like wolves.

What the fuck are they?

I keep pushing, but it's no use; the gap is getting bigger and bigger. Can't hold them off. I've got no foot purchase; my feet keep sliding on the floor tiles. "Shit." They're nearly through. There's too many of them.

I let go of the door and race down the corridor towards the lobby. Looking back, I catch a glimpse of a mob of people bursting through the exit, darting after me. I shoulder the door open and I'm back in the lobby. There's a security guard standing in front of me, eyes wide. "RUN!" I scream at him. Just as I reach the door to the stairs I hear the sound of glass shattering. Turning, I see the entrance doors finally give way to the mass of people.

Shit! It's the alarm!

It's attracted even more of them!

I don't see them storm the lobby; I'm already in the stairwell, galloping up the stairs, taking each step two or three at a time. When I'm two floors up, I hear the ground-floor door slam open and a horde of heavy feet and loud snarls. This time, I don't look back. This time I keep pushing up, ignoring the monsters that I've just unleashed.

Third floor.

Fourth floor. I can still hear them. They're fast.

I see the sign for the fifth floor. I barge through the door and tear down the corridor, heading for room 503. Reaching the door, I bang hard on it, all the while with my eyes locked on the door to the stairwell.

"*Come on, Jen,*" I say through gritted teeth. "*Open the fucking door. It's me. It's Dave.*"

Suddenly the door to the stairwell flies open, followed by a small army of maniacs.

"What's happened?" Jenni asks as she opens the door.

I dive inside, pushing her out of the way as I close the door as softly as I can.

"What's wrong?" she asks, her tone filled with panic.

I shush her as I lock the door, pressing my shoulder up against it. The room falls silent as I listen to the barrage of running feet, of human shrieks, coming towards us like a charge of bulls. I can feel every muscle clench up as I wait for the crowd to start beating their infected fists on our door, scratching at the wood. I look at Jenni as the noises are just outside the door; her eyes are wide, her hands are clasped together, resting on her chin. I know what she's thinking, I can tell.

She's thinking: *What the hell did you do, Dave?*

CHAPTER 7

"What the hell happened?" Jen whispers as the sound of stomping feet vanish.

Still with my ear to the door, I don't answer.

"They're gone," she points out quietly.

"You don't know that. They could be hiding."

Jenni prods me in the shoulder with her fingers. "What happened down there? Did you see the car park?"

I turn to her and then give a faint nod.

"Spit it out, Dave. What did you see?"

I don't answer again.

"*Dave*. Talk to me."

Unable to form the words to tell her how stupid I've been, I bury my face in the palms of my hands, and then slide down the door into a sitting position.

"*Dave*, what's wrong?" she asks, kneeling down beside me. "Talk to me."

After a few seconds, I take my hands away from my face and look at her. "I fucked up, Jen. I really *fucked up*."

"Fucked up what?"

I let out a long exhale, bracing before I speak. "The car park was clear, so I opened an exit door— but then this *fucking alarm went off*. And then these people just kept coming, and coming. Must have been at least ten or twelve. Maybe even more. I couldn't hold them off, so I just ran."

"*Shit.* You let them into the hotel? *Oh my God, Dave.* What have you done?"

"*I know, Jen. I know. I fucked up.* But it gets worse."

"How could it get any bloody worse?"

"As I was running back through the lobby, the glass entrance doors shattered."

"*Jesus Christ.* How the hell did that happen?"

"I think it was the alarm. I think the noise must have rattled them."

"Shit," Jenni blurts out, taking my hand and squeezing it. "How many got in from the front."

I shrug. "I didn't stop to count. All of them I think."

With a look of trepidation, Jenni stands up and makes her way towards the balcony.

The images of those infected people chasing me down the corridor, flood my head; their distorted, twisted features swirling 'round like the after-effects of a horrible nightmare. How could I have been so bloody stupid? Those doors are nearly always alarmed. Why didn't I just check first instead of rushing?

What the hell's wrong with me?

It's Katie. And Clare. That's what's wrong with me. I'm desperate. People's judgement, their actions, always get compromised with desperation, with stress. I just needed to get to them. That's all. No matter what. I wasn't thinking straight.

Anyone would've done the same in my position.

"There's just so many of them, Dave," Jenni says from the balcony, her words laced with fear.

I get up off the floor and head out onto the balcony. The rain has started to pour, but I suppose that's the least of our worries. Jenni is leaning over the railing; I join her. Down onto the dark, wet street, lit only by street lamps and moonlight, I see a horde of people ambling, some running, towards the hotel entrance, clearly aware of its breach. I shake my head in disbelief, knowing full well that I'm the cause of this mess. And most likely the cause of that poor security guard and the receptionist's demise. There's no way they could have avoided all those people storming the lobby like that. No way in the world. Whether I like it or not...I've got blood on my hands.

"What's gonna happen now?" Jenni asks.

"I don't know."

"What do you mean 'you don't know'?" she snaps. "You must have a plan. You're the one with all the *plans*."

"Look, Jen, I don't know. I don't have an answer for everything."

"You do normally. You did ten minutes ago."

"Yeah, but that was ten minutes ago. A lot's changed in that time."

Jenni goes back inside. "So you're saying 'we're screwed' then, Dave?"

I follow her in. "No. I'm not saying that. Keep your voice down. They'll hear you."

"*Then what are we supposed to do then,*" she says, her words broken by a loud sob. "*Because I don't know about you, but I don't wanna die in this room. Okay?"*

I rush over to her and hug her. "We're not gonna die, Jen. I promise."

"You can't promise that."

Taking her by the shoulders, I straighten her body, forcing her to look me in the eyes. "Yes I can. My first plan may not have worked out, but I can tell you one thing: no one's getting through that door. Not if I've got anything to say about it."

"What about your family?"

"Right now, all we've got is each other. You're the only one I need to worry about. Katie is out of my control at this moment. I can't get to her. I'm stuck here. The police will come for us, so we have to sit tight until they do. All right?"

Sniffing, she nods her head. "That's what I said we should do in the first place."

"Yeah, and you were right. I should have listened instead of going out, guns blazing and screwing everything up."

Jenni sniffs again. "Maybe things aren't as bad back in Birmingham."

"Yeah. Maybe. Hopefully."

But as the echoed cries coming from the street below increase, it's pretty obvious that things are far from improved.

I sit with her on the bed, hand in hand, forcing an optimistic smile across my face, all the while feeling these tiny four walls closing in on me, crushing my spirit, my hope, with every second that

I'm not in my car, hurtling down the motorway, heading for home.

I look at Jenni's beautiful blue eyes, her perfect blonde hair, her cherry lips, her young, slender, hourglass figure—and all I can think about is how stupid I was for coming to this Godforsaken hotel in the first place.

This will be the last time I ever see her.

CHAPTER 8

It's been over three hours, and still nothing has changed. The shrieks, the masses, continue to fill the street below us, with their numbers only growing rather than decreasing. God knows how many are inside with such an exposed entrance. Thanks to me. While we've been sitting up against the door, I've heard several people scream. And not the infected kind either. Which can only mean one thing: some poor bastard has opened their door to a swarm of madmen. I don't know if this door will hold them off. But as long as we stay quiet and don't make any heavy movements we should be okay. For now at least.

I've been trying Clare's mobile phone for most of my stint on the floor. But all I'm still getting is a busy network. Best not overuse it. Can't risk the battery dying on me; I'm already down to my last ten percent. Jenni's phone is nearly out too.

I couldn't bear not knowing about the outside world any longer; I had to check the web. Every news article being reported is about this. There is no sports news, no local achievements, and no talk about war, about the budget, about shitty politicians. There's just this: the infection. It's everywhere. And the more I read, the more petrified I am that something dreadful has happened to Katie and Clare. It's so frustrating, so torturous being stuck up here, in this room, away from my family. I swear to God, if I weren't absolutely positive that the fall would kill me instantly, then I'd happily jump off the balcony and make a run for the car. *Any* car. Wouldn't have to be mine. I'd steal the first car that I came across, hotwire it and speed back to Birmingham.

If I knew how to hotwire a car.

The strangest thing about the news reports is the fact that more and more reporters, supposed *professional reporters*, are claiming that the infected are dead. I ignored the first few, but after a while...

It can't be though. It's impossible.

But those infected people, downstairs. There was definitely something lifeless about them. In the eyes at least.

But they were fast. Too fast to be zombies. Zombies are meant to stumble about like, well, like *zombies*. These things were sprinting like they were on drugs or something.

I can feel the weight of Jenni's head against my shoulder. Turning slightly, I see that she's dozed off. I check the time on my phone; it's going on four in the morning. I shake my head, still unable to contemplate how the hell I ended up here and not at home in bed, next to a stunning wife, and my little angel tucked up in bed in the next room.

How did it come to this?

When did I turn into the kind of guy who sneaks out to fuck another woman? It's not me. It's not in my nature. Well, at least it didn't use to be. I should have never gone to that bar. None of this *shit* would have happened. I would have never met

Jenni, and I'd be back in Birmingham. With my family.

Don't talk rot!

I would have never set foot in the shithole of a bar on Boxing Day if things had been better at home. Affairs don't just happen by accident. You create your own problems in life. I may not have asked to be stuck in this hotel room, but I'm the one who put me here! And it wasn't Clare's fault either. She was stuck at home with Katie while I gallivanted around with Jenni, screwing in as many fake courses and seminars as my imagination could muster up. Okay, Clare can be a pain sometimes, a little controlling, but I'm the one who broke that sacred vow. The vow that I never believed in my wildest dreams I would ever break. Just because things have gone a little stale between us, a little lost, doesn't excuse doing something that I'd bet my life on she would never do to me. Not in a million years.

I bet she thinks the same.

The odd thing is though, in some strange, messed up way, I do love Jen. She's smart, sexy, funny—and she's *great* in bed. She's everything a guy could want in a woman. She reminds me of Clare, back in the day. Back before the late evenings stuck in the office, or sleepless nights with a crying Katie, sucked out all the romance, all the spontaneity, all the dreams of travelling, seeing the world, backpacking across Australia. Now all there is to look forward to are family holidays with my sister and my niece, or the occasional night out with friends. And the wild stuff, the adventure, it's disappeared. Watching Katie grow up, being curled up on the couch with Clare—that should be enough. I want it to be enough. But now here I am, sat next to Jenni, and it's pretty obvious that it's *not* enough.

But the grass is always greener. It's a cliché, but it's true. Jenni's a good person, and I love her, really I do. I'm not sure if it's even close to the love I have for Katie, or even for Clare. But I won't leave her here alone. I'll get us out of this mess. But then, once it's over, I'll walk away. Make it work with Clare. I won't ruin Katie's life just because Daddy's going through a midlife crisis. I'll spend more time at home. Go to marriage counselling if that's what it takes. If I can get back what I've lost with Clare, then this nightmare won't all have been for nothing.

"Shit," I mutter to myself when I remember the face of that security guard. What if he's dead? And God knows who else? There were just so many of them.

I drop my head into my hands and groan, trying desperately not to break down and cry. Can't lose it just yet. Got to stay positive.

I look at my phone for maybe a full minute and then try Clare's number again. I nearly crush the phone in irritation when that bloody *network busy* message comes up again. I swallow the frustration like a jagged pill and set the phone down on the floor.

I let out a drawn out sigh and then slowly get up off the floor. Jenni half-wakes. "Where are you going?" she mumbles.

"I'm just going for a pee. I won't be long."

She doesn't answer, just puts her head on the floor, resting it on her clasped hands.

I tiptoe into the bathroom and start to piss in the bowl, struggling to see where I'm urinating due to the lack of light. Not that it matters tonight.

I finish peeing and have to stop myself from flushing the toilet. Force of habit. Stepping out of the bathroom, my heart suddenly jerks in shock.

The sound of a ringing mobile phone fills the room.

My phone!

Terrified that the noise will draw attention to us, I race over to the glow of the phone, which is right by Jenni's head. She shoots up into a seated position in fright. She grabs the phone and hands it frantically over to me. I see Clare's name written on the display. My stomach churns with a mix of emotions; relief that she's still alive, and dread that something awful has happened to Katie.

Just as I'm about to press the 'Answer' button, the door bursts open; large splinters of doorframe fly through the air. Jenni screams as an infected woman storms the room. She pounces on Jenni. Dropping the unanswered phone on the bed, I race over to them, barging the damaged door shut in the process. I grab the crazed woman by the shoulders and managed to pry her off Jenni. The woman throws me a piercing glare and snarls at me, foam dripping from her blood-soaked jaws. She makes another advance on Jenni, so I kick the woman as hard as I can in the mouth; blood and teeth spray over the wall. This only momentarily slows her, and she scurries onto her feet and lunges at me. Slamming my left foot into her chest, she flies backwards, crashing into the door.

"Get to the bathroom!" I shout to Jenni as she cowers against the dressing table. "And lock the door! Now!"

She does what I ask, slipping past me, heading for the bathroom. The woman, still very conscious, charges at me. I move out of the way and she lands on the bed, and then rolls off, hitting her head on the bedside table.

"Come on you fucking bitch!" I say, adrenaline coursing, fists clenched. "I'll kick your *fucking* teeth in! Come on!"

I start to back away as the woman gets to her feet, creeping towards me, her arms out in front, fingers spread. My ass touches the dressing table as she nears me, her grey eyes wide with rage. Reaching blindly behind me, I feel about for a weapon. I hear the sound of makeup items rolling about as I hunt for something big—anything to crack open her skull. But all I find is the hairdryer. I pick it up, holding it by the lead, just a few inches under the handle. I wait until she's a couple of metres from me, and then I swing it, striking the hairdryer on the side of her head. I swing it again. And again, until the hard plastic splits and falls to the carpet. In spite of the blood gushing down the side of her head and neck, she still manages to come at me, still in a full-blown rage. Dropping what's left of the hairdryer on the carpet, I grab her thin wrists, forcing her back against the door, her jaws snapping open and shut relentlessly as if trying to bite fresh air. She's strong, trying to wriggle free from my grasp, so I drive my knee into her stomach. She doesn't flinch. I try again. And again, but still nothing. I try one last time, but she manages to slip out of my clammy grip. She leaps forward, causing me to back away slightly. My feet catch the hairdryer, and I fall backwards onto the floor, taking the woman with me. Pinned down, I just about manage to take hold of her neck and chin, stopping her from biting me. She's getting closer. And closer. Just an inch from my face. I keep pushing, but I'm losing my grip from the sweat and blood seeping through my fingers. The sound of the bathroom door opening distracts her, and she turns to see a horrified Jenni standing in the doorway.

"Get back inside!" I scream at Jenni, but then my hands slip from the woman's chin and she plunges her head down onto the side of my neck, her teeth clamping hard into my flesh. I scream out in pain as I grab her long hair and head, trying to prise her off me. But it's no use; her jaw has locked like a pit-bull.

Just as the room starts to blur through sheer agony, Jenni slams her foot into the woman's head. Rolling off me, she takes a small chunk of skin with her. Scrambling back up onto my feet, hand cupping my bleeding neck, I see Jenni, standing over the infected woman, driving her black heeled boot down into her face, again and again, each stomp harder than the last, as if in a fear induced frenzy. I watch in shock as the woman's face is reduced to nothing more than mush as her head splits open, blood, brains and bone spewing out onto the carpet. I've never seen anything like it. I almost vomit at the sight. I want to tell Jenni to stop, tell her that the woman's already dead, but I can't. I want this *thing* to be gone. I want there to be nothing left of it. But she can't hear me. She's lost in the moment. Away with the fairies.

Fairies with teeth.

Finally, she steps away from the dead woman, staring down at the remains as if seeing them for the first time. She then sits on the edge of the dressing table. I go to her, take her by the hand and then pull her up into a hug, her face buried into my chest. She then lets out an uncontrollable sob. I shush her gently like a baby. "She was gonna kill me, Jen," I whisper to her. "You saved my life. You had no choice. It was self-defence."

I can feel her head nod against my chest. "I know. It's just—"

"Just nothing, Jen. There was nothing anyone could have done for her. She was dangerous. Anyone would have done the same."

She doesn't respond, she just continues to cry into my chest; her head bobbing up and down as the grief consumes her.

After a minute or so, she pulls away, sniffing loudly. "Your neck," she points out. "She bit you. Was it deep?"

I shake my head. "No. Not really. Just a flesh wound. Took some of the skin off, that's all. Don't think she got any arteries. Thank God. I'll be fine. Just need a bandage or something."

"What about the infection?"

Infection.

I completely forgot about the infection. My stomach starts to somersault. I feel sick, dizzy, my vision is hazy. "*Shit.* I forgot. *Oh fuck.*" I go over to the edge of the bed and sit. "I don't feel well, Jen."

"Don't worry, Dave. That's just the shock. There's no way it would affect you that quick. Just get that wound cleaned up and sit tight. I'm sure you'll be all right."

"But they said the virus is spread through bites."

"Yeah, I know, but I'm sure the hospital will have some sort of vaccination for you to take, you know, like tetanus."

"This was not a bloody dog bite, Jen. This one was from a severely infected woman. I'm fucked! I'm a dead man!"

"Look, Dave. You need to calm down. Worrying isn't gonna help."

"I *am* bloody worried, Jen! And so should you be! I'm gonna turn into one of those things!" I point down at the woman, lying dead on the carpet. "I don't wanna end up like that! No fucking way!"

"Look, you need to stay calm and keep your voice down. There could be more of those things in the corridor. And that door is nearly off its hinges."

The room starts to spin. "I think I'm gonna puke."

She sits next to me, placing her palm on the top of my back, rubbing it gently. "Then puke. Let it all out. But it's got nothing to do with the infection. It's just the shock of everything. Just rest up a while." She picks up a towel from the floor and presses it against the bite-mark. "Stressing's only gonna make it worse."

"So I am infected then?"

"I didn't say that."

"But you're thinking it, aren't you?"

"Jesus Christ, Dave, just lie back on the bed and get some rest. There's nothing we can do right now anyway."

The acids in my stomach start to erupt. I turn to the side, away from Jenni, clutching my abdomen. Taking in deep measured breaths, I manage to will the vomit to stay put for a few minutes. But then, like a flash flood, it bursts out of me, all over the carpet, spraying high on the wall. And it keeps flowing until I can barely breathe, barely see. After another few minutes, when there's nothing left in my gut but hot bile, I collapse on the bed, exhausted, delirious. Jenni's words of comfort are muffled, echoed as if at a distance, as if I'm about to fall asleep, or drift into a deep trance. I force my eyes to stay open, to stay focused, but my head is spinning, the room is spinning, out of control like I've just downed a bottle of vodka. I can feel every muscle tighten, and then spasm wildly.

What the hell's wrong with me?

Is it just the shock from the bite? From the attack? From this whole nightmare?

Something drips from my nose, from my eyes. Can't tell if it's snot or tears. Whatever it is feels thick. It runs into my mouth, over my tongue. I can taste it.

It's blood.

"Jenni," I struggle to say, prying my eyelids apart, short of breath. "Where are you? I can't see you."

"I'm right here, Dave. It's all right. Everything's fine."

I can just about see her, sitting opposite on the dressing-table chair, facing me. "I don't feel too good."

She doesn't respond.

"*Jenni!*" I call out, my voice strained. "*I need you.*"

All I see is a churning mess of colours and Jenni's fading silhouette. I'm struggling to focus on her.

I try to keep my eyes on Jenni as she sits there in silence.

"*Jenni,*" I say, my words croaky, barely audible.

She doesn't answer.

"*Jenni,*" I repeat, this time with a little more volume. "*Are you...still there? I think I'm...infected.*"

More silence.

"Of course you're infected," she finally replies, her tone firm, filled with conviction. "And you'll be dead soon."

Did I just hear that? Or did I imagine it?

"Jen. What did…you just…say?"

"I said you'll be dead soon."

"Why did you…say…that?" I ask, trying to get a lock on her blurred figure.

"Because it's true. You'll die, and then you'll come back. Just like that woman did. But I won't be here when you do."

"What are you…talking…about? You said…I'd be okay. You said—"

"I just said that to keep you calm. She bit you, Dave. There's no cure. And there's no help coming for us. If I stay here, I'll die. And I don't wanna die, Dave. Not like this. Not stuck in this hotel room with you."

"Why…are you…saying this…? I love…you."

"No, you don't, Dave. You don't love me, and you never have. I'm just someone to make you feel better about your so-called 'perfect life'. But not anymore. I'm worth more than that. I'm worth more than some hotel-room *fuck*. You're not gonna drag me down anymore. I'm sorry you're dying. But there's nothing anyone can do about it. So I'm leaving."

"Don't say…that…Jen. You're…not…some…fling. You're more…than that."

"I used to think that. But not anymore. So I'm walking out that door, right this minute."

"*But…you'll…die out there.*"

"I'll die in here. And I won't let you hurt me anymore. And I don't think you want that either. So goodbye, Dave… I'm sorry."

Eyes on fire, I watch her silhouette walk towards the door and open it.

"*Please!*"

She stops for a moment in the doorway, but she doesn't respond.

"*Jenni…*"

I hear the door close.

I want to cry, to scream out in anger, in frustration, but I don't have the energy. All I can think about is Katie and Clare, and the fact that I'll never see them again. I think about crawling to the doorway and dragging my body across the corridor, down the stairwell, and into my car, then driving all the way back to Birmingham, back to my home, my family, back to a normal life.

A life that I screwed up.

I close my eyes as the burning sensation courses through my veins. The pain is unbearable, but I'm too weak to react, to cry out. Jenni was right: I'll be dead soon. And I have no doubt in my mind that I'll become one of those madmen.

As the minutes pass by, I slip in and out consciousness, struggling to hold onto any coherent thoughts. I see Katie jumping on her trampoline. I see Clare laughing hysterically as I chase her playfully up the stairs. And then I see Jenni lying next to me, her blonde hair hanging loosely over her shoulders and chest. I gently move the hair out of her eyes and kiss her on the lips.

What have I done?

I can feel something digging into the back of my thigh. I reach under with my fingers and feel something hard. It's my phone. I bring it up to my face and try to focus on the bright screen. It's fuzzy, but I can just about make out the words '*You Have Voicemail*'. Finger trembling, I push the button and lie back, closing my heavy eyes as I listen to the message:

"Dave, it's Clare. I've been trying to call you all day but the network's been down. You're probably aware of what's happened. It's pretty bad down here. They've closed all the schools. But Katie's safe. She's here with me. But she's scared, Dave. We both are. There are people trying to get inside the house. They killed the dog. Katie's very upset. I don't know what to tell her. I've been phoning the police all day but no one's come. It's horrible here. I hope you're safe where ever you are. But come home soon, Dave. We need you so much. I don't know how much longer I can keep them out.

I'm not sure if we'll get another chance to speak before the network goes down again. So I've got Katie here. She wants to speak to you. I love you, Dave. Stay safe. See you soon."

"Daddy, you were wrong. You told me that monsters don't exist... But they do exist. They're real. They're outside. They killed Chloe. And now they want to kill me, too. I'm scared, Daddy. There's so many of them. Where are you, Daddy? When are you coming home? Don't let the monsters get me..."

RUN

Move your ass, Sarah!

I can hear his footsteps, pounding against the damp road just metres behind me. I can hear his groans of hunger, of aggression, as he gains momentum.

But worst of all—I can smell him from here.

I want to rest, take five, give my aching muscles a moment. Maybe I'll be able to stop and hide somewhere soon. I'm sure I'll find a safe place eventually. This country road must go somewhere.

No, I can't. It's not safe. He'll catch me. I'll be a sitting duck. I can't risk it. It's better to keep moving. I'm faster than him. It's only been about four miles. I can do another ten, *easy.* And it's not like it's my first time running this sort of distance. As long as my grinding left knee holds, and my lungs don't burn out, I can outrun him. I'm better than he is. Stronger. More focused.

And for one thing…I'm not dead.

* * *

Why hasn't he given up yet?

Is it just the hunger that drives him? Or is it something more? Something primeval?

As his deep moans get louder, and as we approach around the seven-mile mark, I'm starting to wonder if it's the thrill of the hunt that's the motivation. I mean, none of the other zombies lasted this long.

Is he a wolf? Or a lion? Am I the gazelle?

No bloody way!

The lion always catches its prey. That mouldy bastard's not sinking his teeth into *this* gazelle—gammy knee or not. I'm a winner. A *born* winner. I don't lose. I haven't lost a race since I was eight—and I don't intend losing one today. I throw the pain to the back of my mind and start to gain a little more speed. Glancing over my shoulder, I can see that he's done the same. "Fuck off…you stupid zombie!" I manage to yell between wheezes. "I'm not your dinner! If you want me…you're gonna have to do…better than that!"

I'm sure if zombies could talk he'd be shouting some witty retort like: *'How's your knee, Sarah? Looks painful. Mine feel great by the way. Better than ever. Even better since I passed. And how's the lungs? Those wheezes don't sound too healthy. Mine don't work anyway. Good luck getting to Bedale. I've got all night. And for your information…I can smell you too.'*

* * *

I check the time on my watch: 4:25 P.M. It's already getting dark; that bright orange glow as the October sun descends behind the trees. Moments before it disappears, it always seems like it moves faster than any other time of day. But it doesn't. It's just a trick of the eyes, an optical illusion. Don't know if getting dark will be an advantage to me. But at least the rain has disappeared.

Don't exactly know when this plague started. Maybe a year or two ago. Not sure how it got so bad though; how the government couldn't keep it from spreading. First it was just a few news reports about an infection, nothing major, but then all of a sudden it was on every channel, in every town, city. Most people managed to keep the dead back with large barricades. But that was just a way for us to *think* we were safe. But how can you be safe from death? It's all around us. One bite and within hours you die, within minutes you wake—and within seconds you're off chasing some poor sod down the street, with a newfound taste for human flesh.

It was bad enough that these things could function so well after death…but *running?* No one saw that coming. Crawling, maybe. Ambling, okay, just about. But sprinting like someone pumped up to the eyeballs with amphetamines: Hell no!

We've been pretty lucky in our village; the population's pretty small. Only about three thousand, so infection's been minimal. Most of the larger towns and cities were hit badly though. Especially London and Manchester. The majority of people had to migrate over to the more rural areas just to survive. But that's how infection eventually found us. We were doing fine until they came. We only had about two reported cases. But we couldn't exactly turn the city people away. They were desperate, with young children; some had lost everything—their homes, their loved ones. We had to help. It's easy to look back in hindsight and say we should've put up our own barricades and closed off the village, but that's like saying that you're okay with families being left out to die, to be eaten alive. No thank you. That's not what my legacy will be. I won't become *that* person, no matter how dire things get. We're in this together. 'The Living' versus 'The Dead'. And I plan on remaining on the breathing team.

As long as I can shake off this *fucking zombie!*

* * *

There hasn't been much need for a fitness instructor since the apocalypse. Business has been a little slow. Not like there ever was that much anyway. I've been banging my head against a brick wall for over six years, trying to build a business I could be proud of. I mean, there are plenty of female instructors out there, lots of them making good money. Not me. Not in a sleepy little Yorkshire village in the middle of nowhere. I had to travel all the way to York to pick up a few aerobic classes just to make ends meet. 'Round here, the only clients I'd get were middle-aged women or old-age pensioners, and they only hired me just to help with mobility; most of the time it was the doctor who recommended that they get a trainer. Not that I was complaining. Work was work. But I got into this field because of my passion for running. I imagined myself training local celebrities, top athletes, helping them win marathons, drop several dress sizes, the perfect set of abs—not people who can't even get off the bloody sofa without someone's help.

My knee started going after my second marathon. I've done four of them. I knew I shouldn't have done the last one with my injury. Doctor said it was tendonitis, said it might never get better, unless I went under the knife. To hell with that! I won't let some surgeon touch this body, not after what happened with Uncle David. Messing up a little paperwork is one thing, but taking out the wrong kidney is unforgivable. Poor guy. Died shortly after.

Well, least he didn't have to live through all this shit.

I swore I'd never do another marathon. Twenty-six point two miles is way too far. I know that now. I've learnt the hard way. Just because we *can* do something, doesn't mean we should. Some challenges are only meant for desperate circumstances. Like right now, when you have a bloodthirsty dead man chasing you, with more stamina than any rotting corpse should have.

Now is a perfect time to put all those years of practise to good use.

Every half a mile or so I've been glancing back at him, you know, just to see who I'm dealing with. Well, so far, all I can ascertain is that this zombie is male, mid-thirties, jet-black hair, short back and sides, very slim, with a lean physique. A bit like mine, in fact. Tall and lean: your typical long distance runner. God, maybe he was a runner before he died. It's possible. Maybe that's why he's so bloody fast. *Shit.* I hope not.

Or maybe, *just* maybe, he's slim and lean because he's *dead*.

From the greyish, greenish colour of his skin, I'd say he's been dead for at least three or four days. He's not *fresh,* anyway. Zombies, out in the open-air, facing all of nature's elements tend to rot pretty fast. Not sure if they rot as fast as a real dead body, but I'm guessing, from what I've witnessed over the past few months, close enough. I'm surprised this one has managed to keep up with me, especially with such decomposition. When six breached the community centre and chased me across the field onto this country road, after about half a mile, the other five just gave up and started chasing sheep instead. But this one's different. This one's a fighter. He's got spirit. He's the type of guy that if he sets his mind to something, then he's got to have it. No matter what.

Not even death can slow him down.

Now *that's* what I call dedication.

I wonder what he did, who he was before he got infected. I don't recognise his face, but it's hard to get a good look, what with the grey, lifeless eyes which have no business functioning, buried deep in sunken eye sockets. Jobs have pretty much dried up since the plague, so work uniforms are now a thing of the past. Jeans, royal-blue shirt, stained white trainers don't exactly give away a lot. Being mid-thirties, he's probably married, got a couple of kids out there somewhere.

So sad. To lose someone like that. To see them so distorted, ravaged with decay, with pain. It's not fair. I'm lucky, my mum is safe and sound with my younger brother, and my dad, *well*, he died long before all this started, so at least that's where he'll be staying—six feet under.

Like a normal dead person.

Don't know what I would do if someone I loved was bitten. The experts say you should stab them in the head before they come back. But that's easier said than done. Don't think I could. Haven't even killed a zombie yet. Don't really want to. I'm sure I'll have to—eventually. But even with this one, chasing me, the last thing I want to do is drive a kitchen knife into his temple. But then again, if push came to shove, if it was him or me—then I guess it'd have to be him.

* * *

It's started to rain again; only drizzle though. The sun's almost disappeared, so it's too hard to see how grey the clouds are. TV weather reports are a thing of the past. There's not much call for them since the world fell apart. Hopefully the rain won't get too bad. A heavy downpour is more than likely going to slow me down. Can't say the same for *Mo Farah* behind me though. We're at least nine miles in, and he's still about fifty-metres behind. He's stopped gaining on me, but he's definitely levelled off at a steady pace. Which is only good if I can keep up the stamina, and if this bloody knee holds out.

How long do zombies last?

I mean, if it's a virus, surging through their withered bodies, surely rotten flesh and muscles will shut down eventually. They can't last forever. It's impossible.

Impossible.

That word has lost all meaning since the dead came back to life. Don't think anything will surprise me anymore. What next? World peace? A cure for cancer (although I bet that one's on hold)? Maybe aliens landing? Don't think I'd bat an eyelid if I saw a big flying saucer, hovering down, scooping some innocent man up off the road to take him away for probing.

Knee's really hurting. Don't know how many more miles I've got in me. Really need to rest it, get my weight off it. Wish I'd strapped it up before I started. *Zombies*: so inconsiderate. They could have warned me they were gonna storm the place. I almost never go to the community centre. But Mum insisted. She just had to send me out for supplies. Couldn't she have held out 'til tomorrow? I mean, we weren't exactly desperate. We had eggs, milk, water, and even a little bread. What more do you need?

Just up ahead I see a sign: Ten miles to Bedale. Bloody hell! I can't believe how far I've come. Not sure if the town is safer but at the moment it's the only option I've got. Although, I'm tempted to cut through this field of cows, maybe my deceased friend will change his mind and opt for a little beef instead. It's got to taste better than human. Not that I've ever tried the stuff. Not a fan of beef either, but being a country girl, with sheep and cows all around, in the middle of a zombie apocalypse—fussy eaters don't last very long.

The road is getting slippery. I've got the wrong shoes on for such a long run. Plimsolls were not designed for going the distance. Once again, a big thanks to my dead friend for the lack of preparation time. Hats off to you!

* * *

I've just passed another sign for Bedale: five miles left. My knee is really bad and my pace has slowed quite a bit. The sun has vanished, but the moonlight is strong, in spite of the rain. He's gained some ground; he's now only twenty metres behind. My lungs are still screaming; the cold air isn't helping. And my fingers are white-numb.

Come on, Sarah! Move your bloody ass!

He's not a zombie—he's just some *bitch* trying to steal your glory. He's not interested in your flesh, just the prize. Come on, just a little further. Once you find people, maybe somewhere better than a bush to hide behind, you'll be safe. And this corpse will either be shot down by one of those snipers, or simply join another pack of zombies and forget all about these past fourteen miles of hell.

Or better still, maybe his body will just give up on him. He probably hasn't eaten in a few hours.

Maybe that's all it'll take for him to give up the pursuit.

His strained groans are getting closer as the agony of my knee floods my body again, escaping the back of my mind. Turning my head, I see his face, close up this time; he's even more grotesque that I first thought. His dead eyes even more sunken, his teeth broken, his mouth oozing with God knows what. Spit? Blood? Stomach bile? Whatever it is, it's pretty gross. I think I can even smell it.

I see a junction about a mile ahead. I think I know where I am now. Bedale isn't that far from here. I can make it. Just gotta keep pushing. Keep focused on the finish line.

But my lungs. I can barely breathe…

Forget about your lungs! If that putrid *prick* doesn't need any, then neither do you!

He's so close, just a metre or so away. He's gaining speed. He knows I'm within reaching distance. It's spurring him on. I know that feeling. I've been there so many times. But I won't let him. I *can't* let him. Not now. Not ever. This is *my* race. Not his. I won't let him take away my victory.

I can feel his fingers brushing against my wet shirt. He's too close to turn so I keep pushing forward, trying my utmost not to scream in terror. I won't give him the satisfaction. That's exactly what he wants.

His eager, guttural howls cause me to wince. Haven't had one this near before. Can't stand it.

78

The fear of infection. The sight of such an abomination. The smell of rot.

Let it be your motivation! Not your downfall!

Move, Sarah! You're nearly there! You can do it!

I scream into the cold night air as his fingernails scrape against my back, through the fabric.

I'm done for! I can't make it! He's too quick! I've got nothing left in me.

Let him eat me. I don't care anymore. Just let it be over with.

Chest and lungs bursting, knee hardly bending at all, I drag myself towards the junction. I see a sign, but my vision is hazy; can't read the words. I feel sick. Need to stop. Need to rest. Need water. Sugar.

Just a metre from the sign, my knee gives way, and I collapse, face down, on the wet road, my forehead and palms scraping against the concrete. Scrambling to my feet, I scream out in agony as my kneecap grinds loudly, and then I'm down again. I turn my head, ready to face my victor; ready to feel his teeth sink deep into my flesh; to devour me; to infect me. To take away my trophy.

Let him have it. He deserves it. I'm just a fail—

Where the hell is he?

On my hands and knees, I glance behind me. But he's gone. Vision still blurry, I can just about make out a figure about ten metres away. It's him, lying on his back, staring up at the night sky. Crawling to a standing position, I watch in amazement, the fallen dead man.

He's not moving.

Limping over to him, I watch out for any signs of movement. There are none. When I reach him, I glare down at his emaciated body, his flesh, his clothes, his hair, soaked through. His dismal eyes are wide open; he's looking at me. His fingers are twitching, so are his legs; faintly though, like the last moments before a fish suffocates.

He's dying.

I raise my foot up into the air, hovering my rubber sole over his face, ready to crush his head into nothing more than pulp. His eyes follow my leg, my foot. But he does nothing. All he can do is wait. He wants this. He knows he's lost. He knows I'm the victor.

He looks into my eyes as I raise my knee up even higher. But then he closes them; his legs stop twitching, so do his fingers.

He's dead.

For the second time in his short life.

My foot hangs above his head for almost a minute before I place it down on the road.

"Nice try my friend," I say. "Better luck next time." And then I shuffle away like a zombie, heading towards the junction, back to civilisation.

Today just wasn't your day.

BURNING AMBITION

(First published in Dark Moon Digest. The story has since become a full-length bestselling novel called BURN THE DEAD, published by Black Bed Sheet Books)

It's a dirty job. But someone's got to do it.

Of course, this isn't the first job where my lunch break constitutes a quick sandwich between tasks, or sneaky banana at 3:00 P.M. And it isn't the first job where my working conditions could be compared to the decrepit boiler-room of an 18th Century slave ship. And it certainly isn't the first job where my boss is a sadistic, power-hungry Nazi, content with making everyone's lives as unbearable as possible.

Oh no—I've been here before. I've seen it all, got the T-shirt.

But for me, in spite of everything, life at Romero and Son Limited is complete and utter bliss.

Yes, the long, unsociable working hours are a pain. And yes, being on-call constantly is a major inconvenience—especially with a wife and young boy at home. But waking up every day knowing that you're making a difference in the world—and that no one else has the fortitude or backbone to do it—feels pretty damn good. And for that reason alone, I count myself one of the luckiest men alive.

I just wish it paid a little better.

Another day. Another dollar.

However fulfilling a job might be, nothing feels quite like finishing after a twelve-hour day.

I punch the six-digit code into the panel, and the steel door closes behind me, letting out a face-scrunching squeaking sound as it locks into place.

The late shifts are a killer, especially in the winter. There's something very depressing and *wrong* about starting and finishing work in complete darkness. But it's not like I have much of a choice in the matter. Money is tight all 'round. Vegas is just three short weeks away, and I still haven't saved a penny. And worse still, Tommy is on my back to settle up the flight costs with him.

Walking towards the security guard, whose name I can never remember—three years is definitely too long a time to ask someone's name—I notice the walls in the front hall. *Grey*. What idiot thought of painting them such a bland, depressing colour? Especially in a place like this. Have they always been that colour? *Jesus*.

I pass the guard, giving him an awkward nod goodbye, trying not to make too much eye contact, and leave the building.

* * *

"You're home late, Rob," Anna points out as I enter the kitchen. "How was work?"

"It was fine," I reply, flinging my jacket over the back of the dining chair, and then kissing her on the lips. "Usual stuff. Just a bit tired."

"I bet you are. You eaten yet?"

I let out a fake chuckle. "What do *you* think?"

"So that's a 'no' then I take it?"

"*Yep*. Well, unless you count the bar of chocolate I had at 4:30 P.M."

Anna shakes her head. "That's not right. You should complain to your supervisor. They should hire someone to cover you. Or at least some admin staff. Take some of the paperwork off your shoulders. Doesn't the law say that employers have to give you a break every four hours or something?"

"Probably. But you know what that place is like. Everything's got to be done yesterday. And as for speaking to my boss, I've already tried. We *all* have. It's just in one ear, out the other with him. There's nothing much I can do at the moment. I've just got to suck it up. But the worst thing about it is not taking Sammy to bed. *Again*. I mean, I can handle missing the odd meal and writing up *endless* reports. And I can even handle having a shitty boss. But not spending time with Sammy—it bloody kills me."

"Yeah, I know. Must be horrible. Well, maybe you need to find another job then. Something with more sociable hours. Like a postman."

I let out a small laugh, and then shake my head. "No, it's fine. I'm sure I'll survive. It won't be like this forever. And it *is* a great job. It's just hard sometimes. Like most jobs."

"Well, it's not right." Anna opens the fridge and pulls out a large container, and then places it on the kitchen counter. "Still got some pasta left over. But I wouldn't have this if I were you."

"Why?" I ask, peering down at the chicken, pasta and pesto. "Looks good. What's wrong with it?"

"Well, I had some earlier and now my stomach doesn't feel right. I think I may have undercooked the chicken. Better not risk it. I'll make you something else. Maybe a jacket potato."

"Did Sammy have any?"

"No, luckily. I made him a cheese omelette."

I smile and then shake my head playfully. "What's the point of watching all those bloody cooking shows if you can't even cook a chicken?"

"Very funny," she sarcastically replies. "Just get yourself a shower and scrub that stink off you. Otherwise there'll be no action for *you* tonight."

I smile. "*Action*. Well maybe I don't *want* sex anyway."

"Yeah right," Anna says under her breath.

But oddly enough, and probably for the first time in years, I really don't care either way. I feel completely shattered—from my throbbing head down to my blistered feet (stupid company-issued steel-toecaps boots). But I'm not exactly going to turn down sex, no matter how exhausted I feel.

Seize every opportunity. That's what Granddad used to say.

* * *

I'm lying in bed, waiting for Anna. She's still in the bathroom—vomiting loudly. And she has been for at least twenty minutes. I try to block out the horrid retching noises by turning the TV up ever so slightly.

After another few minutes, I hear the noise of rushing water as Anna flushes the toilet. She then returns to the bedroom.

She looks terrible. Reddened eyes, sweat dripping down her forehead, skin like The Incredible Hulk. She's most certainly seen better days—which is a slight relief seeing as sex is now completely off the table.

"Bloody chicken," she says, as she crawls into bed, sinking deep into the mattress and groaning. "Never again. You can do the cooking from now on. Seriously. I just hope Sammy doesn't suffer the same fate with one of my dinners. Do you think you should sleep in the spare room tonight? Just in case? Don't fancy spewing on you in my sleep."

I shake my head. "Don't be silly. I'll be fine." I kiss the top of her head. "Just don't breathe on me when we're having sex tonight."

"Very funny," Anna groggily replies; too drained even to smile. "At least I haven't got work tomorrow. And if I'm still rough maybe your mother can watch Sammy for a few hours."

"Yeah. Just give her a ring. I'm not working 'til one anyway." I turn to face the other way to go to sleep. "Good night, babe. Just give me a shout if you need anything."

"Okay, Hun. Thanks. Good night. Love you."

"Love you, too."

As I lie there, too exhausted even to sleep, all I can think about, all that races through my overworked mind is: *Please don't be pregnant. Please don't be pregnant. Please don't be pregnant…*

* * *

The toast pops just as a third text comes through from my boss, Stuart.

I mean what's the rush? The delivery isn't exactly going anywhere.

"Hi, Hun," I say, as Anna enters the kitchen, holding Sammy in her arms. She sits him down in his highchair.

"How are you feeling?" I ask her; kissing the top of Sammy's velvet forehead. "Still feel sick?"

"No, just tired. And drained."

"I'm not surprised. Are you going to be okay looking after Sammy this morning?"

"Yeah," she replies. "But I thought you were off 'til one?"

I pull out the two slices of toast and start to butter them. "Had a text this morning to come in early. There's been another problem in Swindon."

"Another? *Jesus*. Isn't that like the third this year? I thought they'd sorted it."

I shrug. "Obviously not. And now I've got to go in 'cause Rich is still off with stress.

Anna clips a bib around Sammy's neck then pulls out a carton of milk from the fridge. "Well, that's what you get for working in a place like that."

I take a big bite of toast, leave the other one on the counter, and grab my jacket from the back of the chair.

Stress. Some people don't know the meaning of the word.

* * *

Slipping the apron over my head, I catch a glimpse of Stuart through the window. I slide my elbow-high gloves on as he enters the room; that smug look on his face; those eyes way too close together, almost becoming one like a Cyclops. He's followed closely behind by two deliverymen, pushing a trolley.

"There's another fourteen outside," Stuart tells me. "So shouldn't take you too long."

"Any details about the inventory, Stu? I mean, any idea how this happened? *Again?*"

"Sorry, Robert, you know I know as much as you do. We get the call, and then we deal with it." He makes his way towards the exit. "I'll see you later. Be careful now. We don't want another incident." And then he's gone.

I spend the next forty-five minutes helping the men offload the remaining trolleys from the truck.

Fifteen trolleys. Not too bad.

The truck pulls away.

Returning to the room, I lock the door. I then approach the first trolley and unclip the steel lid, exposing the thick rubber bag inside. I grab a pair of safety-goggles from the shelf and slip them over my eyes, and cover my mouth and nose with a plastic mask. I gingerly unzip the rubber bag a few inches down to see its contents.

It's another child.

Damn it.

My stomach turns as I pull the zip down a little further to confirm.

It is. The third this month. No more than seven years old. Easily.

Any death is sad—no matter what age. But children. Never children. Children should be out playing on their bikes, not crammed in a Goddamn body bag.

I walk up to the computer panel, turn the dial up to green, then flip the main switch. There's a loud rumble as the furnace ignites. Instantly, I can feel the heat radiate from the sides of the heavy furnace door. The noise circles the room causing the metal trolleys to roll and rattle into each other.

Time to go to work.

Before I wheel the body over to the furnace, I stop to take another look. One last look before someone's child is reduced to nothing more than cinders. I can't help but think of Sammy back at home. I try not to. *God knows I try.* But how could I not think of him? I'm a dad. That's what dads do.

I zip the bag up quickly and start to wheel the trolley over to the furnace door. Opening the heavy door, a gust of eyebrow-singeing heat hits me in the face. I drag the body bag off the trolley and slide it onto the furnace platform. Closing the door forces the rest of the bag inside. I turn the handle and the door locks tight. I press the large red button and the furnace comes alive with fire, burning the body bag and its contents in a matter of seconds.

One down. Fourteen to go.

The next body bag seems a lot more filled-out, which fills me with a quiet relief. I unzip the bag and see the face of a middle-aged man, with blonde, slightly receding hair. I'm not really supposed to open the bags. It's not my job to know—or care for that matter. But something in me always tells me to. I'm not sure why. Perhaps it's out of respect. Or maybe it's just honest-to-God nosey-ness. Either way I have to look. Anna thinks I'm mad. She says that my job would be a lot easier if I just treated the inventory like inventory—and not human beings.

I stare at the man's pale complexion, his red, swollen eyelids, and wonder what he did for a living, when he was…living. Was he a doctor? No, he doesn't seem the type. Maybe a vet? Possibly. Or perhaps he was just a bum like the other twenty percent of the country.

Suddenly his eyes spring open.

I flinch. And then zip up the bag.

I wheel the trolley over to the furnace, ignoring the muffled cries through the thick rubber, and drag him inside. The intense heat hits me again as I prod him with the door until his entire body is safely inside. Pushing the large red button once again, I hear the muffled cries become a crackling sound as the body bag ignites.

Two down. Thirteen to go.

I see that the next bag has started moving already. I pause for a moment and contemplate skipping the face-check.

But I can't resist.

Unzipping the bag, I see the face of another man, this time he's a lot older, maybe sixty, and he's completely bald. His grey, deadened eyes are wide open, and I can hear faint growls behind the muzzle wrapped around his mouth. I wonder what he's thinking. If he thinks at all. If that's a positive thing, the jury's still out, but either way, after all these years I still think of them as people. I can't help it. I know it would make my job a hell of a lot easier, but that's just me. I'm an optimist. Even when the first outbreak happened in Swansea, I believed that these people could somehow be cured; that they were still people underneath all the decay and the God-awful stench of rotting flesh.

But they're dead. I know that now. It's taken me a while, but I do.

And the dead must be burnt.

* * *

I reach the tenth trolley and look at the time. 4:34 P.M. Not bad. With a bit of luck, I'll be home in time for dinner. And I'm starving to death. No lunch break again. Typical. It would be nice if once, just once, Stuart would cover me for even ten lousy minutes for a quick bite. But no, he's tucked away in his nice cosy office, far from the trenches, sipping his herbal tea with a dash of cinnamon.

Prick.

The tenth body is a woman, mid-twenties wearing next to nothing. Was she asleep when she was bitten or was she, in fact, a stripper in the middle of giving some lucky guy a lap dance? I mean, she's got the body for it. And if you look past the muzzle, grey eyes, and bloody gouge on her shoulder, she's not that bad to look at.

This one seems a lot livelier than the others. As I reach to zip the bag back up, I hear a snap. Suddenly I feel a cold hand grab my wrist firmly. Trying not to panic, I carefully begin to pry her grip from my wrist, one finger at a time. Then another hand reaches for me. I leap back in fright, inadvertently pulling the semi-naked woman half-out of the body bag. She's slumped out the side of the trolley. I manage to break free from her grasp but now she's trying to wriggle out of the bag. I race to the furnace, open the door, and then bolt back to the woman who is now almost off the trolley completely. I run to the back of the trolley and push it towards the furnace. The blistering heat is sucking out the air in the room as I ram the trolley into the open door. The force throws the woman into fire. Slamming the door shut, I hear the beating of fists on the furnace walls. I push the large red button, and the woman is no more.

I walk over to the stool and sit; exhausted and shaken up.

Time for a coffee, I think.

* * *

As I finish up the remaining five bodies, I daydream about Vegas. The lights, the booze. That's about it, really. Not much of a gambler. Never have been. More of a watcher. I'll probably have a flutter though, just to say I have.

I slide the fifteenth body into the furnace and push the large red button. A sense of satisfaction washes over me as the blaze inside obliterates the old man.

Done.

I begin to remove my apron. Just as I'm about to hang it up on the wall-hook, I hear the bleeping sound of the code being entered outside. The door opens and in walks Stuart. "We've got another four trolleys for you," he tells me.

"Just four?"

"Yes. It shouldn't take you long."

Sighing, I look outside at the truck, then at the time. 6:07 P.M. There goes another early finish.

When the four are safely inside, I lock the door. Slipping my apron back over my head, I think of Vegas again, and start to count the days in my head. I can almost taste the first beer in the hotel lobby. I lift the lid from the trolley and notice that the body bag is large. I feel relieved as I unzip the bag. It's a woman, no older than twenty-five, and she's chubby. Probably bullied in school. Battled with various quick-fix diets. Had a string of failed relationships. Classic fatty. She stares deep into my eyes; her eyes seem sad. I zip up the bag and throw her in the furnace.

The second body bag is small—not child-small though. This one seems another lively one. I contemplate avoiding the face check but can't resist, ignoring my earlier near miss. I slowly unzip the bag, then stop to make sure there is a muzzle strapped on. There is. Thank God. I continue to pull the zip down to chest height.

It's a woman.

My heart almost stops as I stumble backwards.

Not you.

Please God, not you, Anna.

Choking on my own breath, I creep forward. *Please let it be a mistake.* I pull down my mask and throw off the safety-goggles.

It's not a mistake.

Anna snarls behind the muzzle someone has stuffed into her mouth.

I pull the zip down almost all the way.

She squirms and twists; trying to break free of the restraints someone has fastened to her limbs.

I can barely stand. My knees almost buckle, but I grab hold of the trolley.

Anna is now writhing so much that her trolley has begun to move away from the wall. As I walk over to her, I think of her vomiting last night. How could I have been so stupid; so naive? Why didn't I give her the anti-viral shot—just to be sure? Was I too tired to think straight? Was I too preoccupied with a stupid Vegas trip?

Jesus Christ.

I unbuckle the muzzle and listen to her teeth clack together. The sound goes through me as I consider putting the muzzle back on.

But how could I? I love her. So much. More than anything in the world. And she gave me Sammy: the single greatest achievement of my life.

I walk over to the stool and sit. My stomach is in knots as I listen to her cries of pain and anger. I can't look anymore. It hurts too much to see her like that; a shadow of her beautiful self—her tender, placid self.

It's not you, Anna. It can't be.

It's someone else.

Please let it be someone else…

* * *

I push the large red button, and the furnace ignites. I feel the heat even more so without my mask and goggles. Pushing the trolleys against each other, I listen to the inferno behind me start to die down. I hang up my apron, pull off my elbow-high gloves, and then flip the light switch as I leave the room. I punch the six-digit code into the panel, and the steel door closes behind me, letting out a face-scrunching squeaking sound as it locks into place.

Another day. Another dollar.

It's a dirty job.

But someone's got to do it.

THE PIT

CHAPTER 1

When the lights go out, that's it. The darkness is thicker than anything imaginable. No power. No lights. And through the pitch-black loneliness…The Dead will find you.

I'll be just twenty-five years old next month and already I have seen more death than any man should. Eight long years I have worked in this hellhole; through the dust, the dirt, the claustrophobia. Thelma hates me working down the coalmine, (better known as The Pit), always has done. Even before all this shit started. During my very first week, someone fell from the second lift shaft, broke his neck. Poor bugger died instantly. From the top to the bottom it's a good half a mile. *Easy*. And there are no safeguards up there. Just a giant drop into a black abyss.

Thelma's my wife, and I love her dearly, but I had to take the job. Life on the dole is tough. And jobs don't grow on trees. Work's pretty much dried up these past ten years thanks to Thatcher. And my children, they're still so young. Delith is only seven years old, and Jacob is still just a baby. Can't have them going hungry. Not on my watch. I won't let them live the way I did; broke, with no father, barely a scrap of food on the table, taking handouts just to stay warm. No thank you. Howard John Thomas doesn't take charity. I will always endure, always provide. Yes, The Pit is dangerous, ruthless, and dark—but that's life. Everyone's gotta work. No bloody excuses.

Not even The Dead rising will stop *this* Welshman.

I've had to keep my helmet-lamp off for nearly three hours now. Can't risk turning it back on. Need to save the battery. It's only got another sixty odd minutes of power left. And once it's gone, it's gone. There's no backup battery; they're just too heavy to carry. One hooked to my tool belt is bad enough. The rest of the power's been out since this morning. No tunnel lights. Just the cold emptiness of the black. But the darkness is the only protection I have. There's just too many of them now. They'll find me. They may be slow, and weak, but if there's enough of them, and if you're cornered, without a weapon, then that's it. They'll tear you limb from limb. Most of my friends were bitten, infected by The Dead, endured an agonising death.

But down here…the dead never stay dead.

No one seems to know how all this started, how it somehow spread across most of the UK coalmines. The government, the unions, they're certainly not talking about it. But it's obvious why this all started. Well, it is to me, anyway. We had no business mining so deep. We should have left it alone. Half a mile down is too far. No wonder we pissed him off.

You keep digging deep enough—you're bound to find the Devil.

They're coming. I can smell them. Most of them have been down here for weeks, roaming the tunnels, feeding. Some of them were good men too, now lost to rot and ruin.

The first rumours of The Dead coming back were two months ago. We didn't believe it at first. I mean, who the hell would? We thought that they were merely stories of ghosts, brought on by segregation, fatigue, and boredom. That's why they kept us working down here. No one thought even for a second that the stories were true. But then the disappearances started. Men just lost to the blackness. Search parties were sent down. But once the lights go out, The Pit just swallows you up.

Dennis was the first of my friends to be taken. He said he was off for a piss. When he didn't show for several hours, I assumed he'd fallen asleep somewhere. I mean, it wouldn't be the first time. When our shift ended, Dennis never showed up at the lift, better known as The Cage. A few of us went back for him, but found nothing. No helmet. No tools. Gone. Completely vanished.

That was a week ago. Today, I've seen Dennis twice already.

But it's not him. Not really. It may look like him, if you look past the decay, the hatred, past the colourless, *Godless* eyes. Dennis died that day. Whatever this thing is, it's taken my friend's body. And now it has come for me as well. But I won't let it take me. I won't let them turn me into one of the

Devil's creations. This body is mine. *My* life. *My* soul. No one's gonna take that away from me. I *will* make it out. I *will* make it back to the lift. Back to my family. I'll just have to ration what little power I have left in my helmet-lamp. I'm the last man standing for one reason: I'm a survivor. Maybe Colin made it out; got to one of the lifts safely. He's pretty resourceful, pretty fast for a fifty-two-year-old. He's got a good hour of battery left. And he knows the tunnels better than anyone. He trained me, taught me everything I know about The Pit. Maybe help's already on its way. Word must have got out by now. This curse, this epidemic, it can't be ignored any longer. The people up there have to believe what's down here, what we've unleashed upon the world.

There's no denying it any longer: The Dead walk again.

They've been buried for too long.

CHAPTER 2

I've lost my bearings. I've been heading in the wrong direction for the past two hours. I can feel it in my aching bones. The easiest way back, without any light, is to follow the train tracks. But God knows how I'm gonna find them now. I'm buggered! I'm like a blind man, scrambling through these tunnels, hands running along the cold steel arches that support these crumbling walls, trying to feel my way back to the lift shaft, praying that I don't end up, face to face with The Dead.

So thirsty. I unclip my water flask from my tool belt and take a tiny sip. There's only another gulp or two left. Don't know how long I'll be down here. Have to ration it.

I walk for maybe a mile before deciding to put on my helmet-lamp, just to give me a rough idea where the hell I am. Even with it turned off, the battery tends to drain, so I have to be quick. I push the button and a thick stream of light comes bursting ahead of me.

Light.

I've missed you my old friend.

Maybe another thirty metres in front, I see white stonework. *Thank God!* I think I'm actually going in the right direction. I'm not that far from the rail tracks. I'm sure it's only another tunnel away. Can't be more than ten or fifteen minutes' walk.

If only I could drive the bloody locomotive. It's the only thing that still works since the power died. And I'm guessing she's got at least a half a tank of diesel in her. How hard can it be to drive? She's only small. A couple of buttons, a big fat lever. Easy as pie. If that idiot Jeff can operate the sodding thing, then anyone can.

* * *

I reach the junction. There are three tunnels in front; one leads to God-knows-where, and the other two lead to the tracks. There's a good chance that the train is at one of the two lift shafts. Any one will do; each shaft is only about a hundred metres apart. It'd be a small miracle if the train is still in one of the coal pick-up points. I choose the middle tunnel; I'm almost positive it will get me there quicker. Crossing over the junction, I hear something. *Footsteps*. I freeze, body clenched tightly, heart dashing. Turning my head, I see nothing behind me. I reach for my tool belt to grab my hammer—*but it's not there*. Must have set it down earlier. My screwdriver's missing, too. *Typical*. I cross towards the middle tunnel, but then stop when I hear the noise again. Can't tell which tunnel it's coming from. Think it might be the left one. I brace for a few seconds before proceeding down the middle one.

Without even realising, my light is still on, sapping precious battery life.

"Oh Shit," I whisper to myself, struggling to turn it off fast enough. Just as the light vanishes, I hear a faint groan in the distance.

It's them.

I press forward into the darkness, once again using the wall to guide my path. Most of the tunnels have conveyor belts, stacked with coal, which lead to the tracks. But not these ones. These are the old tunnels; bled dry of coal long before my time. A minute or so passes before I hear the groaning sound again, coming from behind. And more footsteps, slow, shambolic sounding, as if dragging a shattered ankle across the dusty ground. Don't think this tunnel's that far, no more than half a mile, so I keep moving.

I hear a low, rasping voice, just metres behind me.

A cold shudder of panic creeps over me.

They're near.

My pulse soars as I start to move faster, away from the stony sound, away from the smell of death.

The noise becomes a chorus of growls as they close in on me.

Now not even using the walls to steer me, I bolt through the darkness, boots crunching against the loose coal and debris on the floor. I've lost all sense as to how far before I reach the next junction. Can't risk turning my lamp on. I need to find those tracks, or I'm a dead man. Have to make it out. Can't let my family down. I'm not gonna die down here. I won't let The Pit take my—

I crash hard into the wall headfirst.

My body flies backwards on the ground, helmet off my head, lost to the darkness. The battery pack is still attached to my belt, with the power-cable dangling. Head pounding, I scramble about on the floor for the helmet. I can't find it. *"Where the hell's it gone?"* I mutter to myself; tone filled with alarm. *"Come on you bastard. Where are you?"*

To the right of me, about fifty metres away, I see moving lights, at least twenty; a constellation of stars at night. And from the left—more lights. *And behind me, even more.* They're everywhere. What the hell are they?

Shit!

Those are helmet-lamps.

Oh Jesus Christ! They're here!

I give up on finding my helmet and start feeling the wall in front of me, praying that I find the entrance to the next tunnel.

The moans, the footsteps, they're getting closer. *And closer.*

I start to pick up speed as I run my hands over the wall. Where are you? Come on!

Please God. Don't let me die down here. Don't let them take me.

The lights are getting brighter, the howls louder.

I'm done for!

I detach my battery pack from my belt and launch it aimlessly at the lights. I hear it thud against the steel arches. Then I unclip my tool belt from my waist. It's all I have left as a weapon. It'll have to do. I start to swing it wildly through the air, ready to take down anyone who gets too close. Howard Thomas doesn't go down without a fight.

The noise is now deafening. *They're getting closer.*
And closer.
The horde of helmet lamps burning my eyes.
And closer.
And—

Suddenly, as an array of light hits the wall, I see the opening of another tunnel. I sprint to it. Just as I do, a dead man lunges at me. I drive a fist into the side of his face, propelling his withered body backwards against the wall. Then another comes at me, but misses completely. Not looking back, I tear blindly down the tunnel, faster than I've ever gone before. My lungs take in the stale air of The Pit; my heart thunders in my chest. Don't know where I'm running. Don't know where the train tracks are. All I know is that I need to be as far away from those creatures as possible. Even if I die down here, of hunger, thirst, of suffocation, even if I'm poisoned by the methane gas—I won't let them take me. Even with my last breath—*I'll fight to the bitter end.*

After five or so minutes of darting through the gloom, I turn to look behind me, but all I see is more blackness—no lights, no footsteps. No dead men. *Thank the good Lord.* The sweat that's now dripping down my brow, into my eyes is laced with coal dust. It burns. I stop for a moment, catch my breath, and then wipe my eyes with the sleeve of my overall. Trying to preserve what little energy I have, I fast-walk instead.

Thirsty again. Through habit, I reach down for my water flask, but then sigh loudly when I realise that it's gone with the tool belt, lost forever to The Pit. Need to get to one of the lifts soon. If The Dead don't kill me, the thirst surely will. Just got to stay calm. Try not to think about it. Mind over matter.

I can do this.

* * *

Another fifteen minutes of tripping up over loose coal, feeling the wall for guidance, I make it to what appears to be a junction. *Finally!* I go down on all fours, knees digging into the many jagged fragments on the ground, and scurry about for the rail track. Can't feel it. But it must be 'round here somewhere? My hands glide across the floor rubble for maybe another five minutes before I feel something metal. It's smooth, about twelve inches in length and about six in width—with a sharp end. As soon as I'm able to pick it up by its long wooden handle, I realise that it's most definitely *not* the train track.

But it's something almost as good.

Now I have an axe!

A smile slowly forms on my lips; it feels alien, like a madman with a mad plan. But it's the first bit of luck I've had since this morning. And it's long overdue. Brandishing my new corpse-slayer, I start to swing it through the air, imagining taking the head off one of them. Can't think of these creatures as friends any more. My friends are all dead. It's them or me. And now—with the addition of an axe—the odds of this nightmare have dramatically shifted.

CHAPTER 3

I finally locate a tunnel with a conveyor belt, which *must* lead to the track. With my right hand firmly on the axe, and the left stroking the thick, rubber belt to steer my path, I carry on forward, somehow feeling slightly more optimistic about reaching the lift in one piece.

As I make the sightless journey, thoughts of my children flood my mind. I see Jacob, as he lies quietly in his cot, staring up at me with those big blue eyes, studying every inch of my face, absorbing the soft words that leave my lips. And then I see Delith, as she sings her little heart out in the school nativity. So proud of her—even playing a Shepherd. Who the hell wants to play Mary anyway? That's just boring. I see my wonderful Thelma next to me; her thick blonde curls resting on her shoulders, her hand in mine. I smile when she smiles. I laugh when she laughs. The three of us walk to get fish and chips after the play, Jacob asleep in his pram. I finish most of Delith's food. And then I see myself, coming home from a long shift down The Pit. I'm still a little dirty, even after a shower. I chase both my beautiful ladies around the living room, pretending to be a coal-monster. Jacob watches with a smile from his play-mat. Delith laughs so hard she's nearly sick.

This is the life that I have. The life that I've always longed for. And it will be mine again. I don't need light to see. In the darkness, they *are* my light. They *are* my eyes.

And I *will* make it home.

To my family.

I promise…

Just up ahead, no more than forty metres away, I see a small light. Must be another helmet-lamp. I freeze, heart racing once again. I move my hand away from the conveyor belt and squeeze the axe handle with both hands instead. The light is pointing up to the ceiling of the tunnel. Edging forward, one leather boot at a time, I try to make out who the helmet belongs to. I stop, just about ten metres from the light. Through the silence of the tunnel, I hear the distinct sound of gnawing, like a dog with a piece of meat. Edging closer and closer, grip on the axe tightening, I start to see a miner, sprawled out on the floor, his helmet-lamp streaming upwards. *Could it be Colin? Is he hurt?* About two or three metres away, the sound of chewing becomes louder.

"Who's that?" I whisper, axe held up high, over my right shoulder. "Is that you, Colin? It's Howard."

The gnawing suddenly stops dead.

"Who's that?" I repeat, sharper this time. "Answer me."

Skulking nearer, I see someone else. Another man. Kneeling down beside the miner. The light catches the man's face. I see his eyes. Almost all white, with no pupils; sockets deep. And his skin, rotten almost to the bone, receding gums, lips completely absent. And his oozing black teeth—there's something between them. But before I can make out what it is, he opens his jaws and snarls at me with toxic fury.

I jolt in fright.

Gripped with terror, I take a step back with weak knees, ready to turn and sprint as far away as possible. But with nowhere else to go and a horde of monsters still coming from behind, I stop, eyes locked on the creature as he wheezes from ravaged lungs. His thin body starts to straighten as he creeps towards me.

But just before he moves out of the miner's light, I somehow take a step forward, hands trembling, and swing the axe down, driving the sharp steel end into the top of his head. His wasted skull splits down the centre like a piece of stale fruit, spilling blood and gore all over the miner.

Adrenaline coursing through my body, I glare with wide eyes at the mess, unable to comprehend the events of the day. After a full minute, I let out a long exhale to help steady my nerves, and then push the dead man off the miner with my boot. The creature's limp, bony frame slithers onto the ground like hot oil. Crouching down beside the miner, I see a gaping hole in his stomach; his guts spewing out, down his sides and thighs. I remove the helmet from his motionless head and put it on my own. Shining my newfound lamp into his face, I can clearly see that his eyes are shut, and he's just a kid. No older than seventeen. I don't recognise him, but I shamefully thank the good Lord that it's not Colin lying there.

I unclip the battery pack from the miner's belt. *Could use a little water too*. I see his water flask still hooked onto his belt. Reaching for it, I notice a screwdriver—and a hammer. *I'm sorry about this my friend, but I need these*. Grabbing the flask, I suddenly jump back in shock as the miner opened his eyes.

"BLOODY HELL!" I roar, dropping the flask, my voice echoing around the tunnel.

Scurrying backwards, on my hands and knees, I watch in horror as the miner starts to slowly push himself up; even more of his innards leaking out as he stands.

"Oh shit!" I mutter as he groans painfully.

Grabbing the base of the conveyor belt, I pull myself up and start to back away from the infected miner. I let the battery pack hang freely from the cable and then retract the axe. The creature steps a little closer, and then, without a second thought, I plunge the axe-head down into his skull. He drops to his knees, blade still planted firmly in his head, down to his brow. I yank the handle hard, pulling the axe out, taking with it several fragments of bone and skin. And the miner falls face down on the ground.

Dead once again.

Body shuddering, heart pounding, I carry on forward, now with a bright light as a guide—and the blood of two miners at the end of my axe.

* * *

After another mile down the tunnel, I see the junction. I'm tempted to switch off the lamp; especially since I have no way of knowing how much power I have left. But I can't bring myself to do it. It's worth the risk. Don't think I can tolerate another minute down here without light.

At the junction, I point my helmet along the floor. Can't see the tracks just yet. I walk a little further.

"Where the hell are you?"

Just as I'm about to give up and head down yet another endless tunnel, I see something glimmer in the distance, maybe twenty metres to the right. I walk towards it, squinting to see what it is.

When I reach it, when I touch it, when I smell the diesel, I can't stop a giant grin from forming on my face.

The track!

Where the hell have *you* been hiding?

The thirst, the fear, even the claustrophobia— none of that matters now. All that matters is this long piece of rusty steel and following it back to the lift. And out of this stinking hellhole. To freedom.

Judging by the fact that most of the tunnels that I've already been down have been the old, abandoned ones, straight ahead must be the way out. Not sparing a second to argue my logic, I start to jog, struggling with the weight of the axe and battery pack. In my head, I can hear the rumble of the lift as it powers up, heaving the steel cables all the way to the surface, the smell of bad oil, damp, and rotten eggs fading as the bright sunlight fills

The Cage. That feeling of liberation of finishing a hard day's work and stepping back out into the real world. A world of light, of fresh air, of family.

Away from the coal, the steel, the cold air.

Away from The Living Dead.

* * *

I follow the tracks for at least two miles before my lamp starts to flicker. She can't have that much power left in her. Maybe another twenty minutes or so. Hopefully, I won't need it anyway. I've had to give up on jogging. The axe and battery are just too heavy; my shoulders are killing me. But ditching them is the last thing I plan to do. In fact, I may even keep the axe as a memento, to remind me of this day from hell. I can't help but feel that God himself is somehow in my hands—a sword to slay these demons, to rid the world of such abominations.

If the dead can walk, then anything is possible.

I can hear the sound of my bootlace, flapping and dragging against the ground. Going down on one knee, I rest the axe and battery on the floor and start to tie the lace. I exhale in relief as my shoulders take a well-deserved rest. Hate these new boots. They keep rubbing against my ankles.

I finish double-knotting the boot lace. Just as I'm about to stand, I hear footsteps—*coming from behind*. Pulse elevated, I quickly gather up my battery and axe and get back onto my feet. The footsteps seem far. I aim the lamp in the direction of the sound but see nothing, apart from track and steel arches. I continue on forward, only this time I'm running. To hell with my thirst, to hell with my screaming shoulder muscles, ankle blisters. I won't let them get close this time. Not while there's still air in these dusty lungs.

After about half a mile, I have to stop, catch my breath, change hands with the axe and battery. I listen out for the crunching of boots in the distance. Can't hear any. I walk quickly forward, mind locked onto my exit. It's near. I can feel it in my gut, in my bones. I can almost smell the fresh air flowing from the outside world, descending the lift shaft. I imagine Colin greeting me at the top, armed with the military to storm the mine, to purge the tunnels of these creatures. To free the souls of my departed friends.

And to send these *fuckers* straight back to Hell!

My light is fading fast; I'm guessing I've got another five minutes, tops. Have to speed up. I turn to look behind, and an ocean of goose-pimples flood my skin when I see an army of lights, just fifty metres away.

"*Jesus Christ!*" I mutter in terror as I start to sprint; the axe over my right shoulder, the battery flush against my chest like a rugby ball.

Ignoring the pain in my ankle and shoulders, I follow my flickering light. Just up ahead I can see the locomotive. The small train, along with its coal-filled trolleys, has derailed. I clamber through the spilled coal and race to where the driver sits. When I get there I see that the train is empty. No time to figure out what's happened here; have to keep on moving.

The stench of decay fills my nostrils. It turns my stomach. But I'm past caring. I'm almost there. I turn behind me; the pile of loose coal and toppled train has slowed The Dead; their lamps shrinking into the distance. My pace increases. *Liberty is coming.* I see the end of the track. I see empty coal trolleys, loose cable and wood scattered across the floor. I see the discarded sacks of rubble and sheets of steel. I see long wooden benches, and a wall-mounted telephone.

My light cuts off for a moment, but then powers back up. It has barely a minute's worth of light remaining. But I don't need it. I'm here. I've reached the exit.

I've reached the lift!

Thank the good Lord!

I race over to the steel gate that leads onto the lift platform. But the lift isn't there; it's at the top of the shaft. "Shit!"

The lights on the control-panel are out. There's no power going to the lift, and even if there were, it'd be useless; it can't be operated from down here. I poke my head over the gate and peer up the shaft. It's too dark to see anything. But all I'd see is the bottom of the platform.

"HEEEEELP!" I scream, praying my voice travels the half a mile journey straight up. "IS THERE ANYBODY UP THERE?" I listen out for a response, but all I hear is the cold breeze gliding down the shaft. "I'M TRAPPED DOWN

HERE! I NEED THE LIFT SENT DOWN! NOW!"

Still nothing.

"HELLOOOOOO!!!"

Waves of panic wash over me when I'm greeted with more silence.

"Fuck!"

What the hell am I supposed to do now?

Think Howard!

Think hard!

I scan my surroundings, but all I see is useless junk. Nothing to pull me from this nightmare.

"*HEEEEEEEELP!*" I bellow again, this time my voice broken by dread, and anguish.

But then I see something glimmer behind me.

The telephone!

Just as I'm about to dart over to it, to beg them to send help, something grabs my left ankle. I fall down onto the ground, dropping the axe and battery in the process. I frantically reach for the axe, ready to slice open another zombie's skull. Once my fingers surround the wooden handle, once my grip tightens, I kick my ankle free and stand; battery pack dangling by my hip.

But then I stop, almost dropping the axe in disbelief.

"Colin," I say, half confused, half elated. My flickering lamp illuminates his bearded face like a nightclub strobe. *Is he infected? Is he one of them?*

"*Howard,*" he struggles to say; his voice full of gravel like one of The Dead. "*Help...me.*"

Still unsure if he's infected or not, I take a step back. "Have you been bitten?"

"*No.*"

"What happened to you then?"

"*I tried to climb...*" he points to the lift, his finger juddering like an old man, "*the shaft... Lost my...footing.*"

"Where's the lift? When's it coming back for us?"

I hear the faint sounds of The Dead as they roar in the shadows.

Colin slowly shakes his head. "*It's not...coming.*"

"What the hell is that supposed to mean? *Of course it's coming. They wouldn't leave us down here.*"

He shakes his head again. "*They...can't let them...out. It's too...dangerous.*"

The sounds of The Dead are nearing.

I crouch down next to Colin. "There must be something we can do? What about the other lift shaft? Maybe that's working."

"*No, Howard... It's over. They won't...let us...leave.*" He shuts his eyes. "*It's... too late.*"

"Colin?" I say, firmly, shaking both his shoulders. But he doesn't answer. "*Colin? Wake up! Don't you die on me! Don't you fucking die on me! Colin! Wake up!*"

Nothing.

He's gone.

I don't have time to shed a tear.

Time has run out.

They're here.

I stand up, step away from my friend, my mentor, and turn to face the legion of dead miners that surround me. Just before my helmet-lamp fades to nothing, I see the distorted, rotten faces of my enemies; their bright lamps blinding me. Wielding my sword given to me by *God himself*, I throw my helmet to the coal, along with its heavy shackle.

I think of Thelma, and Delith, and Jacob, my parents, and all those people that will never have to face such horrors.

I am a soldier of God now.

A warrior for Jesus Christ.

The devil has come to take me away, to drown me in the blackness of The Pit. If I'm to perish down here today then so be it. I would rather die fighting than allow this darkness to reach the surface. To reach my family.

Next week will be Christmas. But I won't be home. I won't be there to ring in the New Year. 1989 will have to wait. I have important work to do.

The horde of the damned start to move closer, snarling with hunger.

Closer...

But I don't run.

And closer...

Instead, I take my sword with great pride, honour, with the unconditional love of my family.

And I step into the light.

SIMON DUNN: FORMER ZOMBIE

(First published in Dark Moon Digest)

Three weeks in and I'm already outside the boss's office.

The dreaded Mr Prescott.

Third job in two years. I can't keep doing this.

But what choice do I have? It's not exactly my fault. I mean, what's a guy to do: just stand there and let them say those things? Let them put me down?

No thanks. Not me. My father didn't raise a pushover. He didn't spend his time teaching me the importance of morals, strength, and self-pride so that some deranged, self-centred, *bigot* could just walk up to me and call me a *Goddamn murderer!*

No, not *my* father. He believed in standing up for yourself. He taught me better than that. And I'd never let him down. Never soil my father's name. Never soil the *Dunn* name.

Not in this lifetime.

Not me.

I miss him so much.

I really wish I hadn't eaten him.

As I anxiously wait, I notice the secretary glaring at me; her eyes piercing from across the room. She's not even discreet about it. I mean, most people would have the decency to look away when a person spots them gawking, but no, not this one, she's quite content with letting me know *exactly* how she feels about having a Former-zombie work in her office.

Zombie. I hate that word. It fills me with such dread; and even more embarrassment. I prefer walking-dead. Or even coffin-walker. Anything but *zombie.* It just sounds so undignified and low-class. A term coined from crappy old horror movies. A term that conjures soulless and thoughtless monsters, lurching about. But, 'Former-zombie' is now the official and politically correct term for us. I don't know who makes that kind of decision; probably some paranoid politician who's never even *met* a zombie, let alone been one.

God, my life used to be so simple; so…ordinary. I'd get up in the morning, have breakfast, watch TV, kiss the girlfriend goodbye, take the dog for a walk (of course, the dog was the first thing I ate. Start small). Who would have imagined that I'd be one of the three thousand to get bitten that year?

That infamous year. The one everyone now calls, "The year of the dead".

Dead.

It's still a question whether we were ever actually dead at all. Yes, our hearts did not beat, our lungs did not take in air, and yes, our bodies *were* decomposing and had a rotting stench. But dead? That's debateable.

In any event, I'd rather be referred to as dead than a murderer. I'm a good guy! Before that summer afternoon in the shopping mall, before that fat woman bit me, I hadn't so much as returned a library book late, let alone murdered someone. And the experts now say that in order for my body to become fully human again, I must have eaten at least twenty, maybe even thirty humans (apparently dog meat doesn't count). And it's not as if I had any control over my newfound urges—if I had, then I wouldn't have eaten my girlfriend, my parents, my best friend, and God knows who else, now would I?

But what's worse than feeling my body rot, my insides shrivel and die, is the fact that I can still remember eating some of those people; those innocent people. I can even remember the taste.

That putrid, vile flavour that I once hungered for so much. It was like a drug to me; a drug that no matter how much I fought wanting it, I had to have it—even if it meant chomping down on Uncle Nelson's leg.

That was definitely a low point.

And it wasn't as if anyone knew then that we could eventually regenerate if only we ate enough people. It wasn't as if there were courses on the subject, or even a printed leaflet. We former-walking dead fed on instinct. We couldn't help ourselves. We *weren't* ourselves. We were victims of an unknown infection. And seeing as most of the infected were immediately shot in the head and destroyed, there was no way to know how many of us might have finally returned to the land of the living.

Still, we all have to work, don't we? We all have to earn a living—even those of us who used to be dead.

But it's not easy, especially if you have to see the dreaded boss, Mr Prescott. And I'm pretty sure he's not going to go easy on me. Not a chance. He's one scary son-of-a-bitch. And I used to hang around with rotting corpses, so that's saying something.

No, he's not going to do *me* any favours—that's for Goddamn certain.

Especially since I'm pretty sure I ate his wife.

ABOUT THE AUTHOR

Born in the small Welsh town of Llanelli, Steven began writing stories at the age of eight. His inspiration came from his love for '80s horror movies, and novels by the late *Richard Matheson*.

During Steven's teenage years, as well as being a black-belt kickboxer, he became a great lover of writing dark and twisted poems — six of which gained him publications with *Poetry Now*, *Brownstone Books*, and *Strong Words*.

Over the next few years, after becoming a husband and father, Steven spent his free time writing short stories, gaining him further publication with *Dark Moon Digest*: an American horror magazine. His terrifying tales of the afterlife and zombies gained him positive reviews, particularly his story, *Burning Ambition*, which also came runner up in a *Five-stop-story* contest.

Finally, in 2013, after years of hard work and familiarising himself with the publishing industry, Steven got his debut novel, *Fourteen Days*, published by *Barking Rain Press*.

You can find out more about current and upcoming projects by visiting:
www.steven-jenkins.com
Or you can follow Steven on:
www.facebook.com/stevenjenkinsauthor
www.twitter.com/Author_Jenkins

About The Cover Artist

Carolyn Ross is based in Swansea, South Wales. She takes commissions from the UK and overseas, and currently specialises in celebrity portraits. She also takes commissions for a diverse range such as family, children, pets, and illustration work.

She holds a BA Honours degree in fine art painting, and during her degree she specialised in creating large figure paintings in oils.

To find out more about Carolyn, you can visit her website:
www.luciusarts.co.uk

Or you can follow her on:
www.twitter.com/CazzyRoss

OTHER TITLES BY STEVEN JENKINS

FOURTEEN DAYS

Workaholic developer Richard Gardener is laid up at home for two week's mandatory leave—doctor's orders. No stress. No computers. Just fourteen days of complete rest.

Bliss for most, but hell for Richard... in more ways than one. There's a darkness that lives inside Richard's home; a presence he never knew existed because he was seldom there alone.

Did he just imagine those footsteps? The smoke alarm shrieking?

The woman in his kitchen?

His wife thinks that he's just suffering from work withdrawal, but as the days crawl by in his solitary confinement, the terror seeping through the walls continues to escalate—threatening his health, his sanity, and his marriage.

When the inconceivable no longer seems quite so impossible, Richard struggles to come to terms with what is happening and find a way to banish the darkness—before he becomes an exile in his own home.

"Gripping, tense, and bloody scary. The author has taken the classic ghost story, and blended it faultlessly with Hitchcock's Rear Window."

COLIN DAVIES
Director of BAFTA winning BBC's The Coalhouse.

"Fourteen Days is the most purely enjoyable novel I've read in a very long time."

RICHARD BLANDFORD
The Writer's Workshop & Author of Hound Dog

Available at: www.steven-jenkins.com,
Amazon UK, Amazon US,
and all other book retailers.

Robert Stephenson makes his living cremating zombies—a job that pays the bills and plays tricks on the mind. Still, his life is routine until one day his infected wife, Anna, shows up in line for the incinerator, and Rob must cremate the love of his life.

In a race against the clock, he must to find his four-year-old son Sammy, who's stuck in a newly quarantined zone, teeming with flesh-eaters and crawling with the Necro-Morbus virus.

Does Rob have what it takes to fight the undead and put his broken family back together?

Or will he end up in the incinerator, burning with the rest of the dead?

"If you're looking for a fast-paced zombie read, I highly recommend Burn The Dead by Steven Jenkins. His characters have reality and credibility that is often missing from this particular sub-genre of fiction. I found that I really

had an emotional investment in Rob and some of the other supporting characters. Overall, a rip-roaring read, but also thoughtfully crafted and with true heart. (5-STARS)"

K.C. FINN
Readers' Favorite

"*An intense & gripping zombie rush! BURN THE DEAD is an infectious read!*"

HORNS
Author of Chophouse 1 & 2

Available at: www.steven-jenkins.com,
Amazon UK, Amazon US,
and all other book retailers.

SPINE

Listen closely. A creak, almost too light to be heard...was it the shifting of an old house, or footsteps down the hallway? Breathe softly, and strain to hear through the silence. That breeze against your neck might be a draught, or an open window.

Slip into the pages of SPINE and you'll be persuaded to leave the lights on and door firmly bolted. From Steven Jenkins, bestselling author of *Fourteen Days* and *Burn the Dead*, this horror collection of eight stories go beyond the realm of terror to an entirely different kind of creepiness. Beneath innocent appearances lurk twisted minds and scary monsters, from soft scratches behind the wall, to the paranoia of walking through a crowd and knowing that every single eye is locked on you. In this world, voices lure lost souls to the cliff's edge and illicit drugs offer glimpses of things few should see. Scientists tamper with the afterlife, and the strange happenings at a nursing home are not what they first seem.

So don't let that groan from the closet fool you. The monster is hiding right where you least expect it.

"If you love scary campfire stories of ghosts, demonology, and all things that go bump in the night, then you'll love this horror collection by author Steven Jenkins."

COLIN DAVIES
Director of BAFTA winning BBC's The Coalhouse.

Available at: www.steven-jenkins.com,
Amazon UK, Amazon US,
and all other book retailers.